Longarm's h
clothes were covered with dust. Something warm and
wet trickled down the side of his forehead: blood.
Longarm's mouth stretched in a savage grin as he
beckoned with his left hand to the cowboy. "Come
on, old son," he said. "The ball's just getting started."

The cowhand's face clouded up and he lunged at
Longarm with a shouted curse, slugging wildly.
Longarm took one blow in the chest that rocked him.
He turned his left shoulder to the man and bulled in,
hooking his right into his opponent's belly. The man
doubled over in pain, and Longarm brought up his
knee and drove it into the man's face. The man went
backward, blood spurting from his pulped nose.

Holcomb scuttled backward and grabbed for his
gun. "I'll kill you myself—" he gasped.

Longarm's hand flashed across his body to the
cross-draw rig, palming the Colt from its holster with
blinding speed. Holcomb's gun was only halfway out
of its sheath when he found himself staring into the
barrel of Longarm's .44 . . .

DON'T MISS THESE
ALL-ACTION WESTERN SERIES
FROM THE BERKLEY PUBLISHING GROUP

THE GUNSMITH by J. R. Roberts
Clint Adams was a legend among lawmen, outlaws, and ladies. They called him . . . the Gunsmith.

LONGARM by Tabor Evans
The popular long-running series about U.S. Deputy Marshal Long—his life, his loves, his fight for justice.

SLOCUM by Jake Logan
Today's longest-running action Western. John Slocum rides a deadly trail of hot blood and cold steel.

BUSHWHACKERS by B. J. Lanagan
An action-packed series by the creators of Longarm! The rousing adventures of the most brutal gang of cutthroats ever assembled—Quantrill's Raiders.

DIAMONDBACK by Guy Brewer
Dex Yancey is Diamondback, a southern gentleman turned con man when his brother cheats him out of the family fortune. Ladies love him. Gamblers hate him. But nobody pulls one over on Dex . . .

WILDGUN by Jack Hanson
Will Barlow's continuing search for his daughter, kidnapped by the Blackfeet Indians who slaughtered the rest of his family.

TABOR EVANS

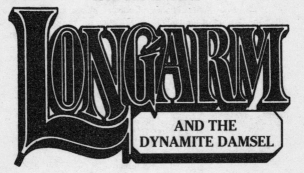

LONGARM

**AND THE
DYNAMITE DAMSEL**

J

JOVE BOOKS, NEW YORK

This is a work of fiction. Names, characters, places, and incidents are
either the product of the author's imagination or are used fictitiously,
and any resemblance to actual persons, living or dead, business
establishments, events, or locales is entirely coincidental.

LONGARM AND THE DYNAMITE DAMSEL

A Jove Book / published by arrangement with
the author

PRINTING HISTORY
Jove edition / March 2000

The Penguin Putnam Inc. World Wide Web site address is
http://www.penguinputnam.com

ISBN: 0-515-12770-1

A JOVE BOOK®
Jove Books are published by The Berkley Publishing Group,
a division of Penguin Putnam Inc.,
375 Hudson Street, New York, New York 10014.
JOVE and the "J" design
are trademarks belonging to Penguin Putnam Inc.

PRINTED IN THE UNITED STATES OF AMERICA

10 9 8 7 6 5 4 3 2 1

Chapter 1

In the darkness of the alley, Rory Pierce leaned back against the wall of the hardware store and smiled in contentment as the whore knelt in front of him.

She was some sort of Scandahoovian, he knew, a farm girl from up in Minnesota who had decided that anything was better than milking cows and slopping hogs and popping out babies for somebody named Sven. Even if that meant spending her days and nights with strangers' cocks in her mouth.

She unfastened the last button of Rory's trousers and reached in to free his shaft. It was only half-erect, and that bothered Rory a little. He remembered a time in his life when it seemed that he was hard all the time. All it took then to get him up was a smile from a pretty woman or a glimpse of an ankle under a swishing skirt. Sure, things changed, he told himself, but why did all the good stuff have to go first?

The whore's fingers closed around him and started pumping. There, that was better, he thought with a sigh. And even better was the feeling the next moment when she leaned forward and engulfed him with her mouth. Her lips closed hotly around his shaft, which was fully erect now. Rock hard, in fact, he thought proudly. At times like this he could forget all about how he was just the town handy-man, barely scraping by with whatever lousy odd jobs folks had for him.

He reached down to stroke the blond hair she wore in a single braid down her back. A little light came into the alley from the oil lamps along the street of the Kansas town. Rory wished it was brighter so he could see her breasts. When they first came back here, she had opened her dress so that he could play with them for a few minutes. They were big, a double handful each, and he had thoroughly enjoyed squeezing the soft flesh and rubbing his thumbs over the thick, rubbery nipples. . . .

Damn, she was good with her mouth. She almost had him ready. His hips started to move back and forth a little, an involuntary motion that was timed with her sucking. Rory gasped, "Here it comes, darlin'!" as he felt himself toppling over the edge. He put both hands on her head to hold it in place.

He caught his breath as his shaft throbbed and began to spasm, spurting his seed into the hot, welcoming cavern of the blond whore's mouth—

That was the last sensation Rory Pierce experienced. The explosion that blew the hardware store into a million pieces was too fast, too violent, for Rory to even feel it as he died.

It was all new enough to him that Jack Bergin was still thrilled to have the job. To wear the badge on his chest and walk the streets of the town and have people look at him with respect, as if he was really somebody instead of just some punk kid. Sure, he was only a deputy now, but one of these days Sheriff Kingman would retire, and by that time Jack would have enough experience to run for the job himself. He would win too. He was sure of it.

Alone in the office on the night shift, he sat at the sheriff's desk going through the wanted posters, studying intently the names and pictures on the dodgers. You never could tell when one of those desperadoes might show up in Little Elm, and Jack wanted to be ready. It was still a while until he had to go walk his rounds, so he leaned back in the sheriff's chair and half-closed his eyes, drifting off into thoughts of what if would be like when that happened.

He would recognize some wanted outlaw and challenge the man, telling him flat out that he was under arrest and that he was being taken to jail by none other than Deputy Sheriff Jack Bergin. If the fella wanted to make a fight of it, so that Jack was forced to draw his Colt with blinding speed and ventilate the ornery son of a bitch . . . well, then, so much better.

Jack laced his fingers together over his belly and sighed. Damn, he was glad he'd decided to stay here in Kansas instead of going back to Texas with the other boys once the herd was delivered.

The explosion made the floor jump. Jack's chair went over backward, spilling him out of it with a yell of alarm.

He rolled over and leaped up, then ran to the door of the office. Without even being aware of it, he had drawn his Colt, and his fingers were tight around the butt of the gun. He threw the door open and bounded out onto the boardwalk to look up and down the main street of Little Elm, unsure of where the blast had come from.

It didn't take long to determine the source of the explosion. A block and a half down the street, Yancey's Hardware—what was left of it—was in flames. Jack broke into a run toward the burning building. On down the street, people were spilling out of the Horsehead Saloon and Casey's Bar, the only two businesses still open at this time of night. Shouted questions filled the air, competing with the crackle of flames to be heard.

Jack was running past Miss Nancy's Millinery Shop when the second explosion hit. The front window of the dressmaker's blew out, sending shards of glass showering over Jack. The force of the blast knocked him ass over teakettle and sent him tumbling into the street. When he came to a stop, he lifted his head groggily. The world had gone quiet. His right ear felt as if a sledgehammer had slammed into it. Something trickled down the line of his jaw. He realized that he was deaf, and that blood was leaking from his ear.

He hurt so bad he wanted to lie there and cry, but that wasn't what courageous Deputy Jack Bergin, someday to be sheriff, would do. So he forced himself onto his feet and looked down at his hand, seeing to his surprise that he was still holding his gun. He turned toward the millinery shop and saw that it too was in flames.

Jack felt the third blast but couldn't hear it. He looked around wildly. Flames shot up from Goble's blacksmith shop, down at the other end of town. Then, before Jack's stunned eyes, the walls of Coleman's Farm Implement Company bulged grotesquely for an instant and then blew outward with incredible force. More flames geysered brightly into the night sky.

Jack started to sob. He couldn't help it. The whole town was blowing up all around him.

And Sheriff Kingman was going to figure out some way to say the devastation was all Jack's fault!

Somebody yelled, and Jack realized abruptly that he was starting to hear things again. The sounds were muffled and distorted, but they were there. His left ear must have started working again, because he was sure that he'd never again hear anything out of his right one.

Instinct made him wheel around, and in the garish light of the fires started by the explosions, he saw the group of riders come boiling out of the alley beside the bank. They were whipping their horses into a gallop, and they wore bandannas pulled up over their faces as crude but effective masks. What looked like full saddlebags were thrown over the backs of their mounts.

Even though he was stunned by everything that had happened in the last few moments, Jack's mind was working well enough for him to know that the bank had just been robbed. He was even able to make the necessary leap of

4

logic and conclude that the outlaws must have set off the blasts as a distraction. If so, the plan was working flawlessly, because right now nobody in Little Elm, Kansas, gave a damn about anything except the fires and the potential threat of more explosions.

Nobody but Deputy Jack Bergin.

Jack raised his gun and stumbled into the middle of the street. "Hold it!" he yelled, only vaguely hearing his own words. The riders didn't slow down, so he squeezed off a shot at them.

Guns flashed in the hands of the outlaws, and Jack felt slugs tearing into him. He was thrown backward but managed to stay on his feet, but he was suddenly too weak to pull the trigger of his Colt. He stayed upright until one of the galloping horses hit him. The animal's shoulder crashed into him and sent him sailing backward. He finally dropped his gun as he landed on his back in the street.

His head was turned toward the bank, so he saw the explosion that ripped through it a second later. The brightness of the blast seemed to sear itself into his eyeballs. In fact, the light got brighter and brighter, even when it seemed like it ought to be fading by now.

Finally, it was so bright that it up and swallowed him whole.

The riders didn't slow their horses to a trot until they were several miles from Little Elm, and they didn't stop to rest the animals until a couple of hours after that. By now the outlaws had pulled down the bandannas that had covered their faces, but the night was too dark for any of their features to be made out.

"You reckon there's a posse after us, Simon?" one of the men asked when the group had come to a halt.

The one called Simon laughed. "Hell, those townies are probably still runnin' around like chickens with their heads cut off. They ain't thinkin' of coming after us. All they're worried about is keepin' the rest of their town from burnin' down. It was all nigh perfect."

"There wasn't supposed to be any killing," another of the riders snapped.

"Well, what were we supposed to do," Simon demanded irritably, "sit there and let that pup of a lawman blaze away at us?" He snorted in contempt. "That deputy knew the risks when he pinned on the badge."

"I still didn't want anyone to be hurt. That's why we planted the explosives in businesses that were closed for the night."

"Listen to me," Simon said, his voice hard. "If you want a line o' work where there ain't no danger of anybody ever bein' hurt, then robbing banks ain't it. Better get that through your head right now, damn it." There was no response from the other, so after a moment, Simon prodded, "Well, what'll it be? You in or out?"

"I'm a bank robber," came the reply. "Let's get going. Just because there's no posse after us right now doesn't mean there won't be one sooner or later."

Chapter 2

Longarm ducked quickly around the corner and put his shoulders against the brick wall of the building. He listened intently, hearing the footsteps of passersby on the sidewalk along Colfax Avenue. He glanced down the alley and wondered if he ought to go hide behind some crates that had been stacked by the side door of the building.

Lord, that it had come to this! Slinking around alleys like he was some sort of ... of ... He was so bumfuzzled he couldn't even finish the thought.

"Ah, there you are, Marshal Long. I thought I saw you as I was coming along the street. What are you doing in this alley?" The voice dropped to a conspiratorial whisper. "Are you pursuing some sort of malefactor?"

Longarm looked at Edward Ezekiel Polk and said, "Uh, yeah, I thought I saw a, uh, a fella we have a warrant out on. Thought he ducked down this alley, but I reckon I was wrong."

"What a shame," Polk said. "It would have been quite enlightening, watching you apprehend a wanted criminal."

"Well, maybe another time." Longarm took a quick step along the sidewalk, saying over his shoulder, "I got to get going—"

"I'll accompany you," Polk cut in, hurrying to keep up

7

with the much-longer-legged stride of the big federal law-man. "Are you by any chance on your way to the office of Chief Marshal Vail?"

There wasn't any chance about it, Longarm thought. He had indeed been on his way to Billy Vail's office when he'd spotted Polk coming the other way along Colfax toward the Federal Building. And the reason he was going there was to complain to high heaven about being saddled with this . . . this little pipsqueak . . .

"Yeah, I'm going to Billy's office," Longarm said through gritted teeth.

"Wonderful. I'd like to thank Marshal Vail again for introducing you to me and making it possible for me to write my article about the exploits of our intrepid federal officers."

Longarm walked a little faster. That didn't seem to bother Polk. He kept trotting alongside, talking his usual mile a minute.

From time to time, Longarm paid a visit to the Denver Public Library. He enjoyed a good book, especially when his wages had already been stretched to the breaking point and he didn't have the necessary funds for drinking or gambling. And for years he'd been flirting unsuccessfully with one of the gals who worked there, sure that if he could ever get her to take off her spectacles and unfasten that ugly bun she put her hair up in and slip out of that shapeless gray dress . . . well, he was certain that the effort would be worth it.

While he was at the library, he sometimes leafed through the periodicals as well, and he had read more than one story in *Harper's Weekly* by somebody called E. E. Polk. This Polk fella wrote about the West, about Indian wars and wagon trains and cattle drives and owlhoots. Seemed to know what he was talking about most of the time too. Longarm enjoyed his writing, even though it was sometimes a mite too colorful.

But Longarm had never dreamed that he would someday

meet E. E. Polk, or that when he did, half an hour later his fingers would be itching to wrap themselves around the journalist's scrawny neck. Billy Vail must have been settling some really powerful grudge when he assigned his top deputy to show Polk around town and answer all of his questions for an article in *Harper's*. Try as he might, Longarm couldn't think of a reason for Billy to have pulled such a trick. Sure, they hadn't seen eye to eye on every little thing since Longarm had pinned on the badge, but still . . .

Polk was a head shorter than Longarm, a narrow-shouldered gent in a gray tweed suit and a bowler hat. Thick-lensed spectacles shielded his weak blue eyes. He was about thirty, roughly a decade younger than the lawman. He talked all the time. His voice wasn't whiny or anything like that; what made it irritating was the sheer never-ending nature of it. And he talked like he wrote too, his sentences full of big words and melodramatic phrasing. So far Longarm had resisted the urge to tell him to shut the hell up, but it was only a matter of time until it happened, he figured.

"I hope Marshal Vail has an actual case for you to investigate," Polk was saying as they started up the steps of the Federal Building. "It would be tremendously exciting to observe your actions in the course of such an assignment. I'm certain my readers would be thrilled to peruse such an account."

"Well, you never know," Longarm said. "Sometimes hell starts popping all over the place, and sometimes folks are downright law-abiding."

"I prefer hell popping myself. Much more exhilarating." Polk laughed. "No one wants to read about people behaving themselves, now do they?"

Longarm didn't know about that. After spending the past few days with Polk tagging along with him almost everywhere he went, Longarm didn't care if he ever read anything else again, especially *Harper's Weekly*.

"You know, I noticed something in the newspaper this

9

morning that I believe would be right up your alley, Marshal. Just the sort of crime you should investigate. It seems that an entire town in Kansas was recently destroyed by a series of explosions."

Longarm stopped short. He hadn't heard about that. He frowned down at Polk and said, "A whole town?"

"Well, in actuality about half of it was destroyed, I believe. And much of the destruction was not due to the explosions themselves but rather to the conflagrations ignited by them."

"You're saying something blew up and started a fire that burned down half the town."

"That's right. As I recall, there were five separate explosions, counting the one that destroyed the bank."

"The bank?" Longarm said.

"Yes, an explosion occurred there too, but not until after it had been looted by the miscreants who were to blame for the destruction."

So there had been a bank robbery too. That sort of made sense, Longarm thought. He had heard of robbers who used dynamite or blasting powder to blow open bank safes. But he hadn't ever heard of a gang that also blew up half the town.

"Where was this?" he asked.

"I'm afraid I don't remember the name of the settlement. I just glanced at the article in the newspaper, you know." Polk's eyebrows went up. "Do you think Marshal Vail might assign you to investigate this atrocity?"

"Don't see how. Robbing banks ain't a federal crime, not unless the thieves steal government bonds or something like that."

"Well, one can always hope, can't one?" Polk gestured toward the entrance of the building. "Shall we go in?"

Longarm nodded in resignation and started up the rest of the steps to the wide porch in front of the entrance.

Before he could get there, the doors burst open and three men in topcoats and derby hats came running out, waving guns around. A couple of women who were nearby screamed. Men yelled curses and ducked for cover. Edward Ezekiel Polk squeaked, "Oh, my."

One of the men had a shotgun in his hands, while the other two were carrying pistols. All of them were bearded. The shotgunner pointed his weapon back into the building and touched off one of the barrels. It bloomed smoke and fire and noise as it spewed its load of buckshot.

Longarm was still half a dozen steps from the top. He moved quickly to the side, putting himself between Polk and the gunmen. In the same movement, he reached across his body for the Colt in the cross-draw rig under his coat. It came out fast and smooth, and he lined the barrel on the shotgunner as he yelled, "Hey!"

One of the other men snapped a shot at him, but firing downhill like that was difficult. The bullet went past Longarm and whined off the sidewalk at the base of the steps. The shotgunner turned to meet the new threat, and as he did so, a .44 slug from Longarm's gun punched through the left lapel of his topcoat and tore on into his body, puncturing his right lung and knocking him off his feet. His finger jerked involuntarily on the trigger of the Greener's other barrel, discharging it and sending the buckshot high into the air. It pattered down onto the street a few seconds later like lead rain.

By that time, the other two bearded gunmen had ducked behind a couple of the thick columns that supported the elaborate portico over the Federal Building's entrance. Longarm called, "Get down!" to Polk as bullets whipped around them.

He heard Polk grunt, and glanced over his shoulder to see the journalist tumbling down the steps toward the sidewalk. Longarm bit back a curse. Billy Vail would really blister his hide if Polk had gone and gotten himself killed while Longarm was supposed to be looking after him. Powering up out of his crouch, Longarm launched himself into a run up the last few steps. He threw a couple of shots

11

toward the columns where the gunmen were hidden, just to keep them occupied.

Longarm flung himself forward onto the building's broad porch, sliding on the smooth stone of which it was made. A bullet chewed chips from right beside him as he went into a roll that carried him behind another of the columns. He was stretched out full-length, shielded from the gunmen.

But if they couldn't get him, he likewise couldn't get them. It was a damn standoff, and Longarm hated standoffs.

He took off his snuff-brown Stetson and edged the brim of it past the column. Almost immediately, a gun cracked and a bullet tugged the hat out of Longarm's hands. It rolled across the porch, a hole in its brim. Longarm grimaced. At least one of those boys could do some fast, accurate shooting.

Gunshots crashed from the entrance of the building. One of the guards inside opened up on the gunmen and tipped the odds. The gunmen had to return his fire, and as they did, the guard retreated back into the building.

Longarm risked a quick glance around the column, and saw what he thought was a topcoat-covered shoulder behind one of the columns across the way. He snapped a shot at it and was rewarded by a yell of pain.

"Toby!" the other man shouted in concern. "Toby, are you all right?"

The only answer was a moan. In all probability, Longarm's shot had knocked the second man out of the fight. He hoped so.

Bells clanging, a police wagon came racketing around the corner. It had taken the local coppers long enough to arrive on the scene, Longarm thought, even though he knew he really wasn't being fair to them. The driver brought his team to a skidding halt, and several blue-coated officers carrying shotguns piled off the wagon.

"Federal marshal!" Longarm bellowed as the barrels of several of the Greeners started to turn toward him. He didn't want to get shot accidentally by some trigger-happy

12

officer. He waved his free hand toward the remaining gun-man. "There's your boy!"

The gunman made the choice easy for the police by opening fire on them. In return, they blasted away at him with the shotguns, forcing him to dart around to the back side of the column to shelter himself from the buckshot.

The only trouble with that was that Longarm had antic-ipated the move and was waiting for him, standing beside the column he had been using for cover. He leveled his Colt at the gunman, who was desperately trying to reload.

"Drop it!" Longarm shouted. "Don't make me kill you, old son!"

The man jammed cartridges into the cylinder of his pistol and snapped it shut with a flick of his wrist. He twisted toward Longarm and started to lift the weapon. Longarm saw the glazed look of fanaticism in the man's eyes, and pulled the trigger of his Colt.

Longarm was trying to put the bullet in the man's right shoulder, but just as he fired, the gunman crouched and moved slightly to the side. The slug took him in the throat instead and hurled him backward. Blood splashed down the front of his coat and sprayed across the porch. Longarm knew from the way the fella flopped that he was already dead.

The Denver police officers charged up the steps and sur-rounded all three of the fallen gunmen. Only one of the three was still alive, the one Longarm had wounded in the shoulder. The bullet had evidently bounced off a bone, ric-ocheted down through the man's torso, and torn out through his groin, because that was where the worst bloodstains were on his clothing. Longarm grimaced as he holstered his gun, walked over, and saw the gore. He'd seen buckets of it in his career, but some things a man just never got used to.

One of the police officers grinned at Longarm and said, "I thought I recognized you. If there's any gunplay anywhere around, you're in the middle of it, aren't you, Longarm?"

"It ain't like I plan my days that way," Longarm said dryly.

"You know who these gents are?"

"Nope, just that they came busting out of the building and waving guns around. The one with the shotgun fired a barrel back inside. I downed him, and then the others started slinging lead."

A new voice said, "I know them." The ring of police parted, and Chief Marshal Billy Vail came through the opening. He was pudgy, pink, and mostly bald, and these days he didn't bear much resemblance to the hard-riding Texas Ranger he had once been, but at moments like this, with a gun in his hand and his eyes hard as flint, it was obvious that not all the bark had been knocked off Billy Vail. "They were trying to get into one of the courtrooms on the second floor," Vail continued. "They're pards of that labor agitator who's on trial for inciting a riot."

"Reckon they must've aimed to start another one," Longarm commented.

"I think they were probably planning to bust him out, but once they saw how many guards we had up there, they panicked and made a run for it. Couldn't resist trying to shoot up the place on their way out, though."

One of the Denver police said, "Damned anarchists."

Longarm slipped a cheroot out of his vest pocket and put it in his mouth. "I don't much care about a fella's politics," he said as he fished for a match, "as long as he ain't shooting at me."

The ring of police parted again for a sawbones who started working on the wounded man. Longarm and Vail turned away, and the chief marshal asked, "Where's Mr. Polk this morning?"

Without lighting it, Longarm dropped the match he had finally found. His eyes widened, and he said, "Oh, hell! I forgot all about him." He started looking around wildly.

14

The last he had seen of Polk, the journalist had been tumbling down the steps of the Federal Building. Longarm didn't know if he had been hit by one of the stray bullets or had simply fallen. A wave of relief washed through Longarm as he spotted Polk standing on the sidewalk and brushing himself off. Longarm didn't see any sign of blood, although Polk's bowler hat had come off, revealing a bald spot in the middle of his scalp. Polk looked up, saw Longarm, and waved his arm.

"Marshal! Oh, Marshal Long!" he called as he started up the steps toward Longarm and Vail.

Longarm turned to Vail with a look in his eyes like that of a longhorn steer spooked by an impending thunderstorm and about to stampede. "Billy, you got to have a case you need to send me on," he implored. "Anything, anywhere, as long as it's away from Denver and that little fella." Longarm suddenly remembered the newspaper story Polk had told him about earlier. "There's a whole town got itself blowed up in Kansas," he went on. "Lemme go find out what happened there." Damn, he hated to beg, but sometimes a man just didn't have any choice. "Please, Billy."

There was a twinkle in Vail's eyes as he rubbed his jaw and pretended to think about what Longarm had said. "A whole town, eh? I'm not sure that falls under federal jurisdiction. . . ."

"Yeah, but wouldn't you like to know what happened anyway?" Polk was almost to the top of the steps, Longarm saw with a nervous glance.

"I reckon it wouldn't hurt to look into the matter," Vail said slowly. "Just in case the local authorities ask us for some help later on."

Longarm nodded eagerly. "Thanks, Billy. I'll go get my travel vouchers from Henry."

Quietly, but with emphasis, Vail said, "Just remember this favor the next time you're thinking about bending the rules, Custis. Or about coming in at noon instead of nine."

"I sure will, Billy. You got my word on it," Longarm

said hurriedly. He broke into a trot toward the building entrance.

"Marshal! Marshal Long! Wait for me!"

Longarm's teeth clenched on the cheroot, and he hurried that much faster.

Chapter 3

The town was called Little Elm, and it stood on the rolling
prairies of western Kansas, at a spot where two creeks ran
together to form a larger stream. At one time, there had
been talk of a railroad spur running north to the town from
the Union Pacific tracks, but that had never come about.
Some good-sized ranches lay to the west and northwest,
and farming country to the east and southeast, meaning that
Little Elm was a supply point for both. Longarm thought
it had probably been a nice-looking town at one time.

Now, of course, half of the settlement was nothing more
than rubble.

Longarm rode in from the south on a bay gelding. He
had taken the railroad most of the way from Denver and
then rented the mount from a livery stable in the flag stop
settlement where he had left the train. He was using his
own McClellan saddle, and his Winchester was snugged in
its sheath. A new Stetson rested on his thick brown hair,
replacing the one that had been damaged during the shootout at the Federal Building. Instead of the tweed suit that
he usually sported while he was in the city, he was wearing
range clothes now, a denim jacket over his butternut shirt
and denim trousers tucked into the high-topped black boots.
His gold Ingersoll watch rested in the right-hand pocket of

his shirt, its gold chain looped across to the left-hand pocket, where the .44-caliber derringer attached to the end of it rode easily. The cross-draw rig carrying his Colt was belted in its usual position around Longarm's lean hips.

He reined in the bay and looked around, studying the destruction. According to what E. E. Polk had told him and the things he had learned since finagling the assignment from Billy Vail, Longarm knew that there had been five separate explosions in the town. Each of them had destroyed one of the buildings and set fire to the ruins. It was difficult to tell, however, exactly which of the buildings had been blown up and which had been consumed by the flames. At least a dozen buildings overall had been destroyed, some at each end of town and some in the middle. The ones still standing were scattered about haphazardly, probably spared by luck as much as anything.

The sound of hammers rang in the air. Rebuilding was already going on in places. Men were clearing away the rubble, unloading fresh lumber from wagons, and nailing together the frameworks of new buildings that would replace those that had been destroyed. Many of the ruins sat empty and desolate, however, the collapsed walls and roofs little more than piles of ashes now.

Some folks bounced back from catastrophe quicker than others, Longarm reflected. No matter how bad things were, they couldn't wait to get back in there and start putting everything to rights again. Others had to grieve and brood over their loss for a while before they could move on and start again. Some never could get over it.

Longarm heeled his horse into a walk, proceeding slowly down the street. He was looking for the sheriff's office, and wondering if it had been one of the structures lost in the blaze, when a young woman walking along the boardwalk caught his eye. She was struggling under the weight of a paper-wrapped package that was obviously heavy.

Without really thinking about what he was doing, Longarm angled his horse toward that side of the street. He had

18

never really thought of himself as chivalrous, and since he was from West-by-God-Virginia he really couldn't be considered a Southern gentleman, but he couldn't sit by and watch a woman having trouble carrying something either.

He reined in, swung down from the saddle, and looped the reins over a hitch rack. As he stepped onto the boardwalk in front of the young woman, he reached up to tug on the brim of his hat. "Howdy, ma'am," he said. "Let me give you a hand with that." Without waiting for her agreement, he reached for the package she was carrying.

She surprised him by pulling back. "No, thank you," she said crisply. "I can manage just fine, thank you."

Longarm frowned. "You sure? That parcel looks a mite heavy for you to be carrying."

As a matter of fact, she was a little slip of a gal and slender in a blue dress. A bonnet of the same color was tied on her blond hair. Her face was both pretty and perky, or at least it would have been if she hadn't been frowning right back at Longarm.

"I'm certain," she said. "Thank you for your kindness, sir." She started to move past him.

Longarm stepped to the side to get out of her way, but a loose plank in the boardwalk suddenly tripped her. She stumbled a little and quickly regained her balance, but not before the paper-wrapped package started to slip out of her arms.

"Oh!" she cried, her blue eyes going wide with horror.

Longarm reacted quickly, reaching out to grab the package before it could tumble all the way out of her grip. He caught it lightly, steadying it, and found her hands touching his as she tried frantically to tighten her grip on the package. "There you go," Longarm said as he took more of the weight until she could brace herself. "I was right. Whatever this is, it's pretty heavy."

"They . . . they're antique glass figurines," the young woman said. "My grandmother collected them." Her complexion had gone as pale as milk, and her eyes were still wide. "I . . . I don't want them to get broken."

"Then you'd better let me carry them," Longarm suggested. He didn't let go of the package. His fingers were still touching hers, and hers were warm.

"All right," she said abruptly. "Perhaps that would be a good idea. Are you sure you have it securely?"

"Don't you worry about a thing," Longarm assured her as he gathered the package into his arms. "This parcel is as safe as a baby in its mama's arms."

"Just don't jostle it, please. You . . . you never know what could happen."

"Where are we headed with it?" he asked.

She pointed down the street toward the far end. "My house is right along there. I'll show you. Be careful."

She was just about the most cautious-natured woman he had ever seen, Longarm thought. Her gait was quick, almost birdlike, as she fell in step beside him while he proceeded along the boardwalk.

"My name's Long, Custis Long," he said, introducing himself.

"Margaret Flynn. Mrs. Margaret Flynn."

So she was married. Longarm said, "Maybe next time you ought to get your husband to carry things like this."

"I . . . don't have a husband. I'm a widow."

"Oh. Sorry." In truth, Longarm really was sorry for her loss, because he wouldn't wish the death of a loved one on anybody. At the same time, the fact that Margaret Flynn was unattached made his interest in her start to perk up again. It had begun to wane when she mentioned that she was a missus. Trying to be polite, he asked, "What happened to your husband, if you don't mind talking about it?"

"I do," she answered.

That left Longarm with no alternative but to say awkwardly, "Well, uh, that's fine." He went on quickly. "Now, whereabouts was your house?"

"That one right there," she said, pointing again to a small frame cottage that sat back a short distance from the street.

It had been whitewashed recently and looked to be in fairly good repair, but Longarm saw a few sagging boards on the porch that most husbands would have fixed right away. That and a few other similar telltale signs were confirmation that there hadn't been a man around there for a while.

"I can take the package now if you'd like," Margaret Flynn offered as she held out her hands.

"No, that's all right," Longarm told her. "I'll carry it in for you. That is, unless you're worried about having a strange fella in your house."

For the first time, she smiled a little. "No, I think you look trustworthy, Mr. Long, at least for the most part. Just be careful when you're going up the steps onto the porch. I . . . I really don't want you to drop the parcel."

"Don't you worry none. I've got it."

She went ahead of him and opened the door, and he carried the package into the house. "Go down that hall right in front of you to the kitchen," she said. "You can put it on the table. Just—"

"I know," Longarm said with a grin. "I'll be mighty careful while I'm setting it down."

He was, and when the package was sitting on the table, which had a white linen cloth draped over it, he stepped back and gave it a solid thump on top. "There you go, safe and sound," he proclaimed.

Margaret Flynn had jumped a little and caught her breath as Longarm struck the package, but she recovered quickly. "Thank you for all your help, Mr. Long," she said. She started to reach inside her knitted handbag. "I'd be glad to pay you—"

Longarm put his hand on hers, stopping her from fumbling around in her bag and as an added bonus getting to enjoy touching her again. "Don't even think about it," he said. Then something on the kitchen counter caught his eye. "But if that's a pitcher of fresh-made lemonade, I'd surely admire to have a glass of it. That'd be payment enough."

"Oh ... I ..." She looked startled by the suggestion. "Yes, that's lemonade, but ..."

"Of course, if you'd rather not ..." Longarm let his voice trail off.

Margaret Flynn laughed, again taking him by surprise. "I suppose you've earned a reward for your gallantry, Mr. Long. Why don't you step out on the front porch, and I'll bring the pitcher and some glasses?"

"I'd be glad to carry the pitcher—"

"No, that's all right. You've done enough carrying for one day. I'll be with you in a moment."

Longarm nodded to her and smiled to himself as he strolled up the hall toward the front door. He hadn't come to Little Elm to meet a pretty woman, of course, and chances were nothing would come of this encounter but a glass of lemonade and a few minutes of pleasant company. But hell, that was nothing to take lightly, he reminded himself.

Still smiling, he stepped out onto the porch, and then stopped short at the sight of the four riders sitting their mounts in the street, facing the house. One of the men was a little in front of the other three, and he demanded angrily, "Who the hell are you, mister?"

Longarm's eyes narrowed as he studied the man. He was wearing an expensive sheepskin jacket and had a broad-brimmed, cream-colored Stetson on his head. The hair showing underneath the hat was a sandy blond color, matching the man's mustache and neatly trimmed beard. He was about thirty-five, Longarm judged. The sheepskin jacket was open, and the walnut butt of a revolver stuck up from a holster on the man's hip.

The other three men weren't worth any more than a glance from Longarm. He pegged them right away as cowhands, judging by their clothes, their boots, and the ropes coiled on their saddles. Hard-faced hombres, all three of them, but the truly dangerous one was the spokesman.

"I asked you a question," the man snapped harshly.

22

"And I ain't got around to answering it just yet, have I?" Longarm drawled.

The man edged his horse forward as his face flushed dark red with anger. "By God, you'll keep a civil tongue in your head, or I'll—"

Longarm's feet moved a little more apart so that he was braced steadily, and his shoulders shifted a little. One of the other riders saw those unobtrusive movements and recognized them for what they were. He leaned forward in his saddle and said hesitantly, "Uh, Boss, maybe you'd best ease up a notch—"

"Shut up, Chris. I know what I'm doing." The man lifted his gloved hands from the saddlehorn and flexed the fingers. "I've got a good mind to teach this saddle tramp a lesson."

Chris straightened and shrugged, his eyes flickering over Longarm. Longarm understood the look. Chris was saying that if his boss wanted to be a damn fool and take on a man who was obviously gun-handy, then whatever happened was on his own head.

Not that Longarm intended to draw on the man. Not unless he had absolutely no choice in the matter. He was here in Little Elm on business, not to get mixed up in some corpse-and-cartridge session where he wasn't even sure what was going on.

"I'll ask you one more time," the man grated. "Who are you, and what are you doing here?"

"I could ask you the same things," Longarm observed coolly.

"That's it!" The man started to swing down from his horse.

Longarm heard a step on the porch behind him. Margaret Flynn exclaimed, "Brad! You shouldn't be here. I told you—"

The man called Brad hesitated when Margaret challenged him, but only for a second. Then he finished dismounting, dropping his reins as he did so. One of the other men

23

reached over from his saddle and caught them, holding
Brad's horse. Longarm could tell from Brad's attitude that
such a response was exactly what he had expected.

Brad stalked toward the porch, saying, "I know what you
told me, Maggie, but I know you didn't mean it."

"I most certainly did! I want you to leave right now."

Brad shook his head and flexed his hands again. His eyes
never left Longarm's face. "Not until I've taught this man
to speak respectfully to me."

"You know, old son," Longarm said mildly, "you've got
a proddy way about you. I didn't come here looking for
trouble, but I ain't in much of a mood to back down from
it neither."

Brad's hands closed into fists. He smiled savagely.
"That's just fine with me."

"Damn it, there's not going to be a brawl on my front
porch!" Margaret Flynn stepped forward quickly, the
pitcher of lemonade in one hand, a tray with two glasses
balanced on it in the other. Brad had called her Maggie,
and Longarm had to admit that the name suited her better
than Margaret. With her face set in angry but beautiful lines
and her blue eyes blazing brightly, she looked like a Maggie.

She brandished the pitcher. "I'm warning you, Brad. So
help me, if you take one more step, I'm going to bust this
pitcher of lemonade over that stubborn skull of yours!"

He stopped, but he looked as if he were more surprised
by her threat than frightened of it. "You wouldn't!"

"Try me," she said in a low, dangerous tone.

With an effort, Longarm swallowed the chuckle he felt
coming on and kept the smile off his face. He had been
threatened with a lot of weapons in his checkered career,
but never by a pitcher of lemonade.

Brad's face twisted in frustration. "Blast it, Maggie—"

"I'll say it one more time, Brad Holcomb. I have no
interest in marrying you, no matter how much you court

me, and I'll thank you to leave me alone and stay away from my house in the future."

"But . . . but my ranch is the biggest one in this whole blamed corner of Kansas!"

Maggie's eyebrows arched. "As if *that* had anything to do with anything!"

Longarm couldn't stop the chuckle this time. "I reckon she's saying that you ain't the most romantic fella in the world, old son."

"Shut up!" Brad snapped. "And stop calling me that. I'm younger than you, and I'm sure as hell not your son."

Longarm chose not to take offense at his tone. He just said quietly, "The lady has asked you to leave. I reckon you'd better do it now."

From horseback in the street, the cowboy called Chris tried again to defuse the situation. "We'd best be goin', Mr. Holcomb," he called. "If we don't get back to the Circle H pretty soon, they'll be sendin' out somebody to look for us."

Conflicting emotions warred openly on Holcomb's face. He didn't want to look like he was backing down, but he was beginning to get the idea that Longarm was not a man to be tangled with lightly. Besides, there was still that pitcher of lemonade looming. . . .

He pointed a finger at Longarm. "This isn't over, saddle tramp. If you're foolish enough to stay around here, I'll see you again."

"I'll be looking forward to it," Longarm said.

Holcomb glared for a moment longer, then turned on his heel and walked to his horse. The rancher's back was as stiff and straight as a fireplace poker. He got on his horse, took the reins back from the man who had been holding them, and wheeled the animal so sharply that it reared up on its hind legs for a second. Holcomb controlled his mount skillfully, then spurred it into a gallop that carried him out of town on a trail that led northwest. The other three riders followed at a slower pace. The one called Chris glanced over his shoulder one last time at Longarm before riding on. Longarm wondered if the fella recognized him from somewhere.

"I . . . I'm sorry," Maggie Flynn said.

And as Longarm turned toward her, the pitcher slipped from her hand, fell to the porch, and shattered into a million pieces.

Chapter 4

Maggie cried out as lemonade splattered across the porch, soaking the hem of her dress. She dropped the tray and glasses as well and stumbled back a step, then started to sag. Longarm reached forward quickly and caught hold of her arms. Shards of broken glass from the pitcher crunched under the soles of his boots as he stepped toward her.

"Mrs. Flynn—Maggie—what is it?" he asked. "What's wrong?"

"I . . . I . . . could you just help me . . . back into the house, Mr. Long?" Her face was pale as milk, and she seemed weak as a kitten. Longarm wondered if she had been suddenly taken ill.

"Sure," he said. "Come on, let's get you inside."

He slid his left arm around her waist and kept hold of her arm with his right hand. She was still unsteady as he led her through the door and into a parlor that opened to the left of the foyer, but she no longer seemed to be on the verge of collapsing. Longarm guided her to an armchair with lace doilies on the arms and back, and she sank gratefully into it. He thought that her color already looked a little better.

"Thank you," she said in a half-whisper. "I . . . I don't know what came over me out there. I suppose it was the

27

strain of dealing with Brad . . . he's been so maddening lately. . . ." She looked up at Longarm. "I'm sorry. You didn't get your lemonade."

"Don't worry about that," Longarm assured her. He thumbed his hat back. "Is there anybody you'd like for me to fetch? A sawbones maybe?"

She shook her head. "I don't need a doctor."

"Looked to me like you were fixing to pass out."

"I'm fine," she insisted. "I just felt faint for a moment. But I'm much better now."

Longarm could tell that. Other than being embarrassed, she seemed to be almost back to normal. He said, "If you're sure . . ."

"I'm certain," she said emphatically.

"Well, then, I reckon I'd better be getting on."

As he started to turn toward the doorway, she said, "Watch out for Brad. He meant what he said, I know he did. He holds a grudge."

Longarm paused. "Is he the sort who'd backshoot a fella?"

"Well, I don't . . ." Maggie thought and then shook her head. "No. No, I don't believe he is. Brad Holcomb is many things, but not a cold-blooded killer."

"As long as he's in front of me, I ain't particularly worried about him."

"But he has a lot of tough men who ride for him. They might attack you."

Longarm smiled. "I reckon I'll just have to take my chances. I've got things to do."

"You're here in Little Elm on business? You're not just passing through?"

She seemed to want him not to leave just yet. And maybe it would be a good idea to talk to her for a while, find out more about the town and its occupants. There might be a connection between Little Elm and the gang of robbers that had wreaked havoc here.

For a second, Longarm considered telling Maggie who

he really was and what had brought him here. After all, he hadn't planned to conceal his identity while investigating the bank robbery and the explosions. But most people talked more freely when they didn't know they were jawing with a lawman, even those who had nothing to hide. In fact, sometimes folks who were innocent were the most close-mouthed of all.

Those thoughts raced through Longarm's mind in the blink of an eye. Then he reached over, picked up a ladder-backed chair that was sitting in front of a writing desk, and turned it around so he could straddle it. He said, honestly enough, "I don't rightly know yet where my business is going to take me, but I reckon I'll be here in Little Elm for a spell. I don't intend to hide from Holcomb while I'm here, though."

"No, I can see that now," Maggie said. "You're not the sort of man to run from trouble. Neither was Tim." She added, "My late husband."

"Timothy Flynn," Longarm said with a smile. "Sounds like a good Irishman to me."

Maggie's smile in return was wistful. "He was a fine figure of a man, so handsome with all that red hair and that dimple in his cheek when he grinned at me. He could look so much like a little boy at times, a mischievous little boy. . . ." Her voice choked off, and tears shone in her eyes.

Longarm tried not to frown. He hadn't counted on this. Like most Western men, a crying woman upset him more than a pack of wolves or a passel of Comanches out for scalps. He said, "I reckon he must've been a good man to have married a woman such as yourself, ma'am."

Maggie shook her head as a couple of tears rolled down her cheeks. She said, "I don't know about that. I think I was a bad influence on him."

"That don't seem very likely to me—"

"It was because of me he wound up in prison," she said flatly. "And if he hadn't been in prison, he wouldn't be dead now."

Longarm didn't know enough of the facts to argue with her. Besides, he hadn't meant for the discussion to become this personal. He had hoped just to ask her a few questions about the raid by the outlaws and the accompanying explosions.

"Sometimes, fellas wind up in prison who don't really belong there," he said, hoping that would be a comfort to Maggie. Although in Longarm's experience, such situations were so rare as to be almost non-existent. Men who wound up behind bars nearly always deserved to be there.

Maggie shook her head again. "No, in the eyes of the law, that was exactly where Tim belonged. He was a bank robber, you see."

Longarm tried to conceal his surprise. "Really?"

"Yes. And I'm to blame. Tim always felt like he couldn't give me the things I wanted by working at an honest job." She smiled sadly. "He never realized that all I really wanted was him."

Longarm didn't see how the fact that Maggie's late husband had been a bank robber could be connected to the trouble that had brought him to Little Elm, but he filed it away in his head anyway. You never knew when some scrap of information might prove to be valuable. He asked, "What happened to your husband in prison?"

"He was . . . killed . . . by one of the other inmates. Stabbed. With a homemade knife. I don't really know why. I . . . I suppose I'd prefer not to think about that."

Longarm didn't blame her, and he didn't intend to stir up any more bad memories. Instead, he changed the subject by asking, "How long has Holcomb been bothering you?"

"Brad? At first he wasn't really a bother. He was a friend. When Tim was arrested and put on trial and sent to prison, Brad didn't turn his back on me like so many of the people in town." A note of bitterness entered her voice as she went on. "I was good enough to teach their children how to read and write, but not good enough to speak to or even nod to on the street. Brad might have used his influence to help me—as he said, he *does* own the largest ranch in this part of the state—but I wouldn't let him. If he forced people to accept me again, it wouldn't be real."

Longarm could understand that feeling. He could also make a pretty good guess about what had happened next.

"So after your husband was killed, Holcomb decided it was time for you and him to be more than friends?"

"Not right away," Maggie said. "Not even Brad is that crude. He allowed me a few months to . . . to grieve. Then he simply announced that he thought he and I ought to be married. I would be better off out at the Circle H head-quarters than I was here in town, he said."

"Like I said before, a real romantic hombre," Longarm observed with a smile.

"I'm not interested in romance," Maggie said crisply. "But Brad couldn't understand that. He's been badgering me ever since to marry him, and I've been refusing him. It's gotten to be so much of a strain that I've ordered him to stay away from my house and not even speak to me. And then . . . and then today . . ."

"Reckon I can see why you were upset," Longarm told her. He tried to steer the conversation back onto topics that held more interest for him by asking, "How long have you lived here in Little Elm?"

"Three years. It's been a little more than a year since Tim was sent to prison, and eight months since he . . . died."

"So you must know most of the folks in town."

"Yes, of course. Not everyone, but most of them, what with teaching school and all."

Longarm nodded. "I could see when I rode in that there'd been some trouble here."

Maggie looked slightly surprised as she asked, "You hadn't heard about it?"

"Nope. Some sort of fire by the looks of the damage, wasn't it?"

31

"Fires caused by half a dozen explosions," Maggie said grimly.

Deliberately, Longarm lifted his eyebrows. "Explosions? You mean somebody set 'em off and started the fires on purpose?"

"It appears that way, because the bank was robbed too." A humorless laugh came from her. "Perhaps I should be glad Tim is dead; otherwise the townspeople might be blaming him for *that* too."

"Don't say that," Longarm told her. "But I sure am surprised to hear about what happened. Cleaned out the bank, did they?"

"Yes, and killed a poor young man named Jack Bergin too. He was the deputy sheriff on duty that night. The outlaws gunned him down mercilessly."

Longarm clucked his tongue and shook his head. "Damned shame. Anybody else hurt?"

"Well . . . two people disappeared that same night, and it's thought that they might have been killed in one of the explosions, even though their bodies were never found. One of them was the town handyman, and the other one was a, ah, soiled dove."

Longarm nodded. It was certainly possible that the two missing people might have been blown to bits by one of the blasts. Even more likely if they had been together at the time, and considering the profession of the woman, that was possible too. He said, "I'm sorry to hear about that. Does anybody have any idea who those owlhoots were?"

"Not really. And with everything that was going on here in the town, the fires and everybody not knowing if another explosion was going to go off at any minute, it was hours and hours before Sheriff Kingman was able to gather a posse and go after them. The next morning, in fact."

"They didn't find the gang?"

"I heard there were some tracks, but they disappeared in the hills southwest of here. The ground gets rather rocky there, I've been told."

"Is this sheriff of yours still looking for 'em?"

Maggie looked slightly puzzled, as if the question had never occurred to her. "You know, I don't have any idea. I suppose it sounds callous of me but, well, since my house was spared, I haven't kept up that well with anything that's happened since the night of the explosions."

Considering the way the town had treated her, Longarm wasn't surprised that she was not overly concerned about the aftermath of the raid. He said, "I imagine those blasts shook your place pretty good, though. You're not that far from the center of town."

"I thought it was an earthquake at first," she said with a faint smile. "Either that or the end of the world."

Longarm didn't figure a bank robbery qualified as apocalyptic, even with dynamite involved.

Maggie went on. "Thank you for staying here and talking to me, Mr. Long. I feel much better now. I'm still very annoyed with Brad Holcomb, but at least I don't believe I'll faint now." She stood up. "In fact, I'd better go sweep up all that broken glass on the front porch."

Longarm got to his feet. "I can do that if you'd like," he offered.

"Absolutely not. You've already done more than enough, and I appreciate your great kindness. It's not often that a perfect stranger is so considerate. I'm just sorry you never got that lemonade."

"Another time maybe," Longarm suggested.

Maggie hesitated, but only for a second. Then she said, "Yes, another time perhaps. I think I'd like that."

Longarm was still thinking about Maggie Flynn a few minutes later as he tied his horse at the hitch rack in front of the sheriff's office. The squatty stone building appeared to be untouched by the fire.

Maggie was attractive enough, but Longarm recalled a bit of advice he had heard often as a young man: Never get involved with a woman who has worse troubles than you do. He figured that she wasn't really completely recovered from the murder of her husband, not to mention the circumstances of his death and the fact that the townspeople had treated her so badly. Plus she had the problem of Brad Holcomb to deal with, and the arrogant rancher had struck Longarm as the type who wouldn't take no for an answer when he wanted something, no matter how many times he heard it.

Besides, Longarm was here on a job, not to spark some pretty little widow woman. That, and to get away from E. E. Polk, Longarm had to admit if he was being honest with himself.

The journalist had been very disappointed that he wasn't going to get to come with Longarm on this case. "Sorry," Longarm had told him curtly. "The Justice Department's got its rules, though, and we can't cross Uncle Sam."

"Well," Polk had suggested, "perhaps we can get together when you get back to Denver, if I'm still here. How long do you think this mysterious assignment of yours is going to take?"

"No way of knowing," Longarm had said, mustering up as much sincerity as he could. "Could be weeks, maybe even months."

"And you can't tell me where you're going or what you're going to investigate?"

With a shake of his head, Longarm had begun, "Those pesky Justice Department—"

"Rules, I know," Polk had concluded with a sigh. Then he'd stuck out his hand. "Well, I wish you good luck, Marshal, and Godspeed."

Longarm had felt a mite guilty shaking his hand after Polk had expressed that heartfelt sentiment. But only a mite.

Now, as he stepped up onto the boardwalk and crossed to the door of the sheriff's office, he was glad he'd left Polk back in Denver. By now, Polk would have told half the citizens of Little Elm and the surrounding vicinity that

Longarm was a famous United States marshal, and Longarm had decided that it might be more profitable to play his cards close to the vest for a spell.

He opened the door and stepped into the office. With a pleasant nod, he said, "Afternoon," to the lean, white-haired, walrus-mustached gent behind the desk. "You the sheriff?"

The man pushed himself to his feet. "Sheriff Jonas Kingman," he confirmed. A big revolver rode in a holster on his hip. Longarm recognized it as an old Dragoon Colt. Kingman went on. "What can I do for you, son?"

It had been a while since anybody had called Longarm "son" without another word that rhymed with "itch" following closely behind it. Kingman had fifteen or twenty years on him and was clearly a veteran star packer. Longarm didn't know if he could fool the sheriff or not, but he said, "I was just passing through, Sheriff, and saw that you'd had a heap of trouble here. Mind telling me what happened?"

"You got any reason why I should?" Kingman shot back suspiciously.

The idea leaped unbidden into Longarm's head, and the next thing he knew, he was saying, "I'm a journalist, thought there might be a story here. Name's E. E. Polk. I write for *Harper's Weekly*."

Kingman frowned. "Hell, son, no offense, but you look more like a saddle tramp than a reporter." He gestured at Longarm's .44. "Right down to that hogleg."

"You know how it is out here on the frontier, Sheriff," Longarm said easily. "A fella can sometimes run into trouble whether he's looking for it or not. That's why I carry this gun. As for being a reporter, I can wire my stories in from anywhere there's a telegraph office, so I don't have to stay in any one place."

Kingman grunted, then nodded his head in acceptance of Longarm's story and waved a hand at the chair in front of the desk. "Sit down, Mr. . . . Polk, was it?"

"Edward Ezekiel Polk," Longarm said.

"Huh. Quite a mouthful," Kingman said as he lowered himself into his chair once more.

It certainly was a mouthful, Longarm thought. Not only that, but he had already introduced himself to Maggie Flynn as Custis Long. That was all right, he told himself. If the question of his real name ever came up, he could always tell her that Polk was just a phony moniker he used for his writing, like a swindler using an alias so people wouldn't know who was stealing from them.

Longarm sat down in the uncomfortable, straight-backed chair and asked the sheriff, "You ever read *Harper's*?"

"I ain't got much time for readin'," Kingman said, and that was a relief of sorts to Longarm. "Got even less time since some no-good skunk of an owlhoot killed one o' my deputies."

"Was the deputy being killed part of the trouble that burned down half your town?" Longarm asked, even though he already knew from Maggie what had happened to Jack Bergin. He just wanted to get Sheriff Jonas Kingman talking.

Kingman did so, spending the next ten minutes telling Longarm basically the same story he had already heard from Maggie Flynn. The sheriff concluded by saying, "I can't prove it, but I'm convinced a couple more folks died in one o' those explosions. A no-account fella named Rory Pierce, did odd jobs round town, and a Swedish hoor called Elsa. She was always takin' fellas back in one o' the alleys to toot on their harp, and I wouldn't be a bit surprised if they both got blowed to kingdom come." The lawman's thin lips curved in a slash of a smile, and his face suddenly reminded Longarm of a vulture. "Reckon Rory probably got blowed twice that night."

Longarm put aside the instinctive dislike he felt for Kingman and asked, "Were you ever able to get a hint of who pulled off the robbery?"

Kingman shook his head. "Nope. There was a trail of

sorts, but it petered out 'fore we could even come close to catchin' up with those boys. I don't like it, but I don't know what else to do. They're long gone."

Longarm thought the sheriff was probably right. He didn't much care for Kingman's attitude, however. Giving up and letting a bunch of killers get away rubbed Longarm the wrong way. He had begged this case from Billy just to get away from Denver by himself for a while, but now that he had arrived in Little Elm and heard the full story for himself, he found that he was angry at the brazen ruthlessness of the outlaw gang responsible for the explosions. From what he'd heard, Jack Bergin had been a decent young man and a promising peace officer. The other two people who had probably been killed in the raid, the handyman and the soiled dove, would have been considered less important by some folks, but not by Longarm. *Any man's death diminishes me,* one of those old English poets had written, Longarm recalled, and while he wouldn't have gone quite that far, he still felt a sense of outrage and injustice at the deaths here in Little Elm. Just like for Jack Bergin, the bell shouldn't have tolled for Rory Pierce and Elsa either.

Just like that, Longarm reached a decision. The matter of jurisdiction might be pretty shaky, but he didn't care.

He was going to find the sons of bitches who had come to Little Elm carrying flaming hell in their fists.

Chapter 5

Longarm spent a few more minutes shooting the breeze
with Sheriff Kingman, but didn't find out anything else
worthwhile. As he stood up to leave the sheriff's office,
Kingman asked him, "Going to be around Little Elm for a
few days, are you?"

"More than likely," Longarm said. "I like to write about
the places I visit, so I'll probably scribble down a few stories while I'm here."

Kingman stood up and shook hands with him. "Well, if
I can be of any help to you, Mr. Polk, you just let me
know."

"I'll do that," Longarm promised, but he figured he had
already gotten everything out of the local lawman that he
was likely to.

He paused in the doorway as a thought occurred to him,
however, and looking back at Kingman, he said, "One more
thing. I ran into a fella called Holcomb. What can you tell
me about him?"

"Brad Holcomb?" Kingman arched his bushy white eyebrows.

"That's him," Longarm said.

"Why, Brad owns the Circle H. Big spread northwest of
here. Biggest in this part of Kansas, I'd say. His father

started the ranch, and when old Dave died a few years ago, Brad took over. He's made the place even more successful. A fine young man, just fine."

Longarm nodded. Kingman had told him what he wanted to know: The sheriff was firmly under the thumb of Brad Holcomb. If Longarm had any more trouble with the rancher, it was unlikely he would be able to look to Kingman for any help. Chances were, no matter who started the fracas, Kingman would blame anybody but Holcomb.

That was all right; Longarm was used to stomping his own snakes anyway. But he liked to know where he stood, and now he did.

He left the sheriff's office and started down the street, getting a feel for the town—or what was left of it. He saw a short man with massive shoulders clearing debris from around a stone pedestal with an anvil mounted on it, and figured the man was Little Elm's blacksmith. In front of another destroyed building, someone had pounded a stake into the ground and nailed a hand-lettered sign to it: *Gone back to Pennsylvania. Any damn fool who wants what's left can have it.*

At the edge of town, Longarm crossed the street and started back up the opposite side. He was going to need a place to stay while he was here, so when he came to the only hotel he saw, he stepped into the lobby, which was small but well kept.

The man behind the desk nodded to Longarm and said, "Good afternoon to you, sir. What can I do for you?" He was about Longarm's age, with fair hair, a long face, and slightly prominent teeth that were revealed by his friendly smile. He was wearing a gray suit, a white shirt, and a string tie.

"Need a room, I reckon," Longarm said.

"Of course." The man turned the register around and plucked a pen from an inkwell. "If you'll just sign the book . . ."

Longarm took the pen. Normally he would have just

scrawled either his own name or Custis Parker, that being an alias he often used because Parker was actually his middle name, but since he had already laid some groundwork with the sheriff, he carefully wrote *E. E. Polk* in the hotel register, then added, *Denver, Colorado*.

The man behind the counter was obviously skilled at reading upside down, because he said, "Welcome to the Thorne House, Mr. Polk. We promise not to stick you." The man chuckled at what was obviously an old and often used witticism. He extended his hand. "I'm Carl Thorne."

Longarm shook with the man and said, "Own the place, do you?"

Thorne laughed. "And sweep it out too. Will you be staying with us for long?"

"Don't rightly know. I'll pay for the room for a couple of nights." Longarm intended to try to pick up the trail of the bank robbers, but he'd be using Little Elm as the starting point of his search.

"That'll be two dollars then," Thorne told him. Longarm reached into his pocket and brought out a couple of coins. He dropped them into Thorne's outstretched hand. "I'll put you in Room Three. Right up those stairs over there, and it's on the front. Nice view of Main Street." A shadow passed over Thorne's face. "Not that there's much to look at these days except a bunch of ashes."

"Looks like the fire spared this place, though," Longarm commented.

"And I've been thanking my lucky stars for that ever since it happened," Thorne said. "I was on my way back to town that night, and I saw the flames from miles away. Nearly lashed my buggy team to death hurrying back here, I'm ashamed to say. By the time I arrived, most of the fires were under control, and I was relieved to see that the hotel hadn't suffered any damage."

"Lucky," Longarm agreed. "I'll need a place to put my horse."

Thorne nodded. "Chambers' Livery was destroyed, but I

40

have a corral out back of the hotel here. It's a little crowded these days, but if you want to use it, you're welcome to. Need any help with your bags?"

"Nope, all I've got is a pair of saddlebags and my rifle."

At the mention of a rifle, Thorne glanced down at the Colt holstered just ahead of Longarm's left hip. His tongue came out and touched his lips briefly, and then he said, "What, ah, line of work are you in, Mr. Polk?"

"I'm a reporter," Longarm said as he turned away from the desk. He was going to keep up that masquerade as long as he could.

Thorne seemed to be chewing that over. Longarm didn't say anything else, just went back out of the hotel and headed for the hitch rack where he'd left the rented horse. He untied the animal and led it around to the corral behind the hotel.

The corral already had about a dozen other horses in it, but Longarm didn't think his mount would be too crowded. He unsaddled, then put his gear in a shed beside the corral. Gathering up an armful of hay from a bin inside the shed, he took it into the corral and used a couple of handfuls to rub down his horse, dropping the rest of the hay onto the ground so that the occupants of the corral could nibble on it. He stepped back out and swung the gate shut, throwing the bolt that held it closed.

"There you are."

Longarm didn't turn around for a second. He didn't have to. He recognized the voice. When he finally did swing around slowly, he saw Brad Holcomb and two of the cowhands who had been with him earlier. There was no sign of the one called Chris. The three men stood about twenty feet from Longarm, in the open space between the corral and the back of the hotel.

"Thought you went back to your ranch," Longarm said.

"Not yet," Holcomb replied. "Since he didn't have any stomach for what's coming, I sent Chris back to let the rest of the boys know there's nothing to worry about."

41

"Did you tell him to draw his time and ride on too?" Longarm asked, thinking that was exactly what a man like Holcomb might do to an employee who didn't support him one hundred percent.

"Of course not. Chris is a good hand. He's just too soft-hearted for his own good sometimes."

"Not like you."

Holcomb sneered. "I know what I want, and I'll stomp any man who gets in my way into the dirt."

"What you want is Maggie Flynn," Longarm said.

"Damn right. I mean to have her too."

"Whether she wants you or not."

Holcomb flicked a hand. "I told her earlier, she doesn't really know what she wants. But it's not you, saddle tramp." His eyes went to Longarm's horse. "You might as well get that nag back out of the corral. You're not staying here in Little Elm."

"Last I heard, it was a free country," Longarm drawled.

Holcomb's voice hardened even more. "Not for you. You're riding on right now, and you're not ever coming back here."

"Or . . . ?" Longarm prodded.

"Or we bust you into little pieces first, and then you still ride on. It'll hurt a hell of a lot more that way, though." Holcomb started forward, slowly closing the distance between himself and Longarm. "What'll it be, saddle tramp?"

Three to one odds, Longarm thought. He had faced worse before and come out on top. But there was a chance he wouldn't this time, and if he didn't, Holcomb and the other two men would hand him a vicious beating. Longarm had no doubt of that.

Of course, he could always draw his Colt. None of the three men were gunslicks; Longarm could tell that by looking at them. Holcomb was probably the fastest, and Longarm was confident the rancher couldn't shade him. Holcomb would probably try, though, and Longarm didn't want any gunplay. Not over this.

"Better think this over, Holcomb," he advised. "Tangling with me isn't going to make Maggie like you any better, or agree to marry you."

"She'll come around," Holcomb said as he clenched his fists. "Sooner or later, she'll see that the best thing for her is to go along with what I say. And it'll be sooner without some meddling son of a bitch like you around to distract her."

Longarm didn't plan to do any distracting or anything else with Maggie Flynn. He had liked her immediately, and he wouldn't mind sharing that glass of lemonade with her sometime in the future, but that was as far as his thoughts had gone.

Holcomb had closed to within arm's reach. His hands were balled into fists. "You had your chance, saddle tramp," he said. He swung a looping punch at Longarm's head.

The blow was telegraphed, and Longarm's knees bent as he ducked under it. Holcomb was trickier than Longarm had given him credit for, however, and the first punch was nothing but a feint. Holcomb's left shot out in a swift jab. Longarm tried to block it, but the punch slipped past him and landed solidly on his chin. His head rocked back from the impact.

Holcomb closed on him with a flurry of punches. The rancher's fists thudded into Longarm's midsection. Longarm stumbled back a step, off balance. That lasted only a second. He planted his left foot and then stepped forward with his right, at the same time throwing a right cross that had all the power of his arms and shoulders behind it. His fist slammed into Holcomb's jaw and sent the rancher flying backward.

"Get the bastard!" one of the cowhands yelled. He and his companion surged forward.

The second cowboy tackled Longarm, driving him back and off his feet. Both of them fell, but Longarm twisted on the way down so that his opponent landed first. Longarm's weight came down on the man, and whiskey-laden breath gusted out into Longarm's face. Holcomb had obviously taken his men to the saloon and liquored them up before coming to look for Longarm.

Longarm rolled, neatly avoiding a kick that the other cowboy aimed at him. As he came to his feet, he saw that Holcomb was still down, lying on his side and shaking his head groggily. The rancher might get back in the fight, but it would take him a few more seconds before he regained his senses. The man Longarm had fallen on was still gasping for air after having the wind knocked out of him. That made the odds even, if only for the moment.

Longarm's hat had come off in the fracas, and his clothes were covered with dust. Something warm and wet trickled down the side of his forehead: blood, no doubt, from a cut opened by one of Holcomb's punches. Longarm's mouth stretched in a savage grin as he beckoned with his left hand to the other cowboy. "Come on, old son," he said. "The ball's just getting started."

For an instant, the cowhand looked as if he wished he were somewhere, anywhere, else at this moment. But then his face clouded up and he lunged at Longarm with a shouted curse, slugging wildly.

Longarm took one blow in the chest that rocked him, but he managed to avoid all the others. He turned his left shoulder to the man and bulled in, hooking his right into his opponent's belly once, twice, a third time. The man doubled over in pain, and as he did so, Longarm brought up his knee and drove it into the man's face. The man went backward, blood spurting from his pulped nose.

Hearing the shuffle of footsteps over the hammering of his own pulse, Longarm spun around to meet the charge of the other cowboy, who had caught his breath and finally gotten up. Holcomb was still on the ground, but was sitting up now, and as his man charged at Longarm, he shouted, "Get him! Kill the bastard!"

The cowboy tried, but his heart wasn't in it. Longarm blocked his punches and landed a couple of his own, including a solid right just under the heart that made the man's face go ashen. He stumbled back, tripped, and sat down hard. Longarm could have gone after him, but didn't. He turned instead toward Holcomb.

The rancher was still on the ground. Longarm said, "I seem to recollect you saying something about being stomped into the dirt."

Holcomb scuttled backward and grabbed for his gun. "I'll kill you myself—" he gasped.

That made it a whole new story. Longarm's hand flashed across his body to the cross-draw rig, palming the Colt from its holster with blinding speed. Holcomb's gun was only halfway out of its sheath when he found himself staring up into the barrel of Longarm's .44. From that angle, the muzzle of the gun must have looked as big around as the mouth of a cannon.

"Don't," Longarm said quietly.

Holcomb's fingers came off the butt of the revolver. Already halfway drawn, it slipped from the holster and thudded onto the ground, raising a little puff of dust. With a stubborn vestige of his earlier arrogance, Holcomb said, "You kill me and you'll swing for it. I swear you will."

Longarm doubted that, but he supposed it was possible, given Holcomb's wealth and influence in the area. It was really a moot point, though, because he wasn't in the habit of shooting anybody who was unarmed. "Get up," he snapped. "I ain't going to kill you. I told you right from the first that I wasn't hunting trouble, Holcomb."

Holcomb got shakily to his feet and glared at Longarm. "I find you sniffing around my girl, what was I supposed to think?"

"First of all, Miss Maggie ain't your girl, and if you'd just listen to her, you might get that through your thick skull. Second, I wasn't sniffing around her. When I rode into town I saw her having trouble carrying a heavy package, and I gave her a hand with it. She was going to give

45

me a glass of lemonade for helping her. That's it. That's all. You understand now, Holcomb?"

But even as the words left his mouth, Longarm saw the taut line of the rancher's jaw and the way Holcomb's eyes still blazed with anger and hatred. Holcomb wasn't going to listen to reason. He wasn't going to listen to anything.

Longarm eared back the hammer of the Colt.

"If you ain't heard anything else I've said, hear this: You come after me again and I'll kill you," he grated, his voice low and grim. "Simple as that. You leave me alone, and I'll leave you alone."

"What about Maggie?" Holcomb challenged.

"That's up to her." If Holcomb wanted a competition, then by God, Longarm would—

He stopped that thought. He had come to Little Elm on business, he reminded himself, even if his motivation in coming had been a little on the shaky side. Getting into a pissing contest over some gal should have been the last thing on his mind.

Holcomb had forced the issue, though, and Longarm wasn't about to let anyone try to draw on him and get away with it.

"Go on now," he said. "You and your boys get out of here. I don't figure to tell you again."

Holcomb bent over and picked up his hat, then reached for his fallen gun.

"Nope," Longarm said sharply. "You can come back and get it later, when I'm gone. Right now, just leave it where it lays."

Holcomb looked ready to argue, but he slowly straightened and left the gun where it was. He knocked the dirt off his hat and put it on. Without even glancing at the two men he had brought with him, he turned and walked away through the alley that led alongside the hotel.

The two cowboys had picked themselves up and brushed themselves off. They hesitated until Holcomb was halfway up the alley, then started after him. One of them mumbled under his breath to Longarm, "No hard feelin's, mister."

"The hell there ain't," Longarm said.

He waited until all three of them were out of sight before he holstered his gun. Then he sighed and picked up his own hat. It had gotten trampled on during the fight. Remembering the shootout on the steps of the Federal Building back in Denver, as he tried to knock the Stetson back into shape, he wondered why he was having such bad luck with hats these days. Of course, it was better for his hat to get a bullet hole in it than his head, he reminded himself, and a Stetson could be molded back into shape a lot easier than a fella's skull. Maybe he wasn't having such bad luck after all.

That made him think of Maggie Flynn, and although he knew it was unwise, he suddenly found himself wondering what she was doing for supper tonight. He remembered his vow to keep his mind on business, not on this unwanted rivalry with Brad Holcomb.

But hellfire, one little supper couldn't hurt anything . . . could it?

Chapter 6

The Thorne House had a back door, so after retrieving his Winchester and saddlebags, Longarm went in that way in hopes of avoiding any curious stares regarding his disheveled state and the cut on his forehead. He found a narrow staircase just inside the door and used it to climb to the second floor. He followed a hallway to the main landing and went from there to Room Three. The door of the hotel room was unlocked.

He went in and looked around. The room was similar to hundreds of others he had seen, on the smallish side and furnished plainly with an iron bedstead, a couple of chairs, and a table containing a pitcher of water, a basin, and a folded cloth. The single window was covered by a yellow curtain that had been pulled back halfway to let the sunlight in. Everything was spick-and-span; either Thorne or his wife or housekeeper liked things kept neat.

Longarm leaned his rifle in a corner, dropped his saddlebags on the bed, and took off his jacket and shirt. He shook them out, then draped them on the bed as well and went to the table to wash the dust off his face. He soaked the cloth in the basin and winced as he dabbed at the cut on his head. The cloth came away red. There was no mirror in the room, so Longarm couldn't see how bad the wound was, but he could tell by the feel of it that it wouldn't require stitches.

By the time he had cleaned up enough to feel presentable again, his stomach was reminding him that it was late afternoon and he hadn't eaten since breakfast on the train that morning. He put his shirt and jacket back on, carefully settled his hat on his head, and left the room. As he eased the door shut, he took a stub of matchstick from his pocket and placed it between the door and the jamb, low down so that nobody would be likely to notice it. He locked the door, but locks could be opened. The matchstick would give him a little extra warning if anybody went into his room while he was gone.

Carl Thorne was still behind the desk when Longarm reached the lobby. Thorne was smiling again as he said, "Why, Mr. Polk, I didn't see you come in after you left a while ago."

"I put my horse in the corral and then came in the back door," Longarm told him.

Thorne's smile disappeared as he noticed the injury on Longarm's forehead. "What happened to you?"

"This little scratch?" Longarm gestured toward the cut. "Banged my head on the corral gate as I was closing it."

A look of worry came over Thorne's face at those words, and Longarm figured the hotel owner was wondering if his guest would somehow try to blame the hotel for the mishap. Longarm eased that fear by adding, "It was my own blamed fault. Wasn't watching what I was doing close enough."

"We have a competent doctor in town, if you'd like to pay him a visit," Thorne suggested. "His name is Munson, and his office is right down the street."

"He didn't get burned out?"

"He was another of the lucky ones," Thorne said.

Longarm shrugged. "I don't reckon I need a sawbones, but if I do, I'll keep that in mind. What about a place to eat?"

"There's a pretty good hash house called Dooley's, a block down and on the other side of the street. We had a

49

fine restaurant here in town, but unfortunately, it was lost in the fire. And there's Casey's Bar too. Casey always has pickled eggs and such-like for his customers."

Longarm felt the need of something more substantial, and if he was going to ask Maggie Flynn to eat with him, he sure as blazes wasn't going to invite a lady such as her to a saloon. He nodded and said, "Thanks. I'll give Dooley's a try."

He left the hotel and went looking for the hash house to check it out before he walked down to Maggie's. Spotting the establishment where Thorne had said it was, he started toward it, but before he got there he noticed Maggie herself coming toward him on the boardwalk. She didn't have a package this time, but she had tied the blue bonnet over her hair again.

They met in front of Dooley's, and Maggie said, "There you are, Mr. Long. I was looking for you."

Longarm didn't bother correcting her as to his name, since there was no one around whom he had introduced himself to as Polk. He just smiled and tugged on the brim of his hat and said, "Well, here I am, big as life and twice as ugly."

"Oh, not ugly at all, I'd say," Maggie responded instantly. "But I'd have to agree about the other part. You're definitely a big man."

She sounded almost coquettish, Longarm thought, as if she were flirting with him. Well, maybe she was, he told himself. Nothing wrong with that.

"I was just about to rustle up some supper," he said, inclining his head toward the door of the hash house. "Care to join me?"

"That's why I was hoping I'd run into you again. How does a home-cooked meal sound to you?"

Longarm had already noticed the smell of old grease coming from inside Dooley's, and a glance through the flyspecked window of the place showed him a dingy interior populated by grim-faced cowboys and farmers and

50

townies who seldom even glanced up from their food.

"A home-cooked meal sounds mighty fine," he replied honestly, "especially if you're the one who's going to be cooking it, Miss Maggie."

She smiled at him and linked her arm with his. "Indeed I am," she said. "Come with me then, Mr. Long. I promise you a meal you'll enjoy more than what Mr. Dooley can provide."

Longarm didn't doubt that for a second. The company would be a lot more pleasant too. That was for damned sure.

Maggie seemed to be completely recovered from her nervous, fainting state earlier in the afternoon. Since she didn't mention Brad Holcomb, neither did Longarm, but during their walk to her house, he had noticed several of the townspeople giving them fishy stares. Maggie might be something of a pariah in Little Elm, but the townspeople had to be aware of Holcomb's interest in her. Longarm was willing to bet that someone would tell the rancher all about how the stranger in town had walked down to Maggie's house and had dinner with her.

He supposed he ought to warn her that this dinner invitation might lead to trouble for her once Holcomb found out about it. The rancher wouldn't actually hurt her, Longarm felt sure of that, but he would probably show up sooner or later and start browbeating her again. Of course, he was liable to do that anyway, whether Longarm had dinner with Maggie or not, so Longarm decided, at least for the moment, not to spoil things by bringing up Brad Holcomb's name.

With evening coming on, the sound of hammering from the rebuilding efforts had stopped. Even after all this time, however, there was a faint smoky smell of ashes in the air to remind Longarm of what had happened here in Little Elm, as well as the actual destruction itself, which was still very visible. Longarm and Maggie had to detour around several burned-out stretches before they reached her house.

"Too bad the men who did this got away," he commented.

"Yes, it is. But I don't want to think about that this evening." She looked over at him and smiled. "I'd rather we just concentrate on enjoying each other's company."

"Sounds like a mighty fine idea to me," Longarm agreed.

When they reached her house, she ushered him into the small parlor and took his hat. As she did so, she frowned at the cut on his head. "What happened there?"

"Little run-in with a corral gate," he said, using the same lie he'd told Carl Thorne. He felt a mite guilty about not telling Maggie the truth, but he had already decided to leave Brad Holcomb out of things as much as possible tonight.

"Wait here," she said. "I'll be right back."

She bustled out of the parlor, leaving Longarm to look around at the neatly kept, well-furnished room. He hadn't paid that much attention to his surroundings when he was in the parlor with Maggie earlier in the day. At the time, he had been more concerned with whether or not she was going to pass out. Like the rest of the house, the parlor was nice, although nothing fancy, but he noticed a tiny crack in the wall that needed patching, and one of the floorboards moved under his foot as he ambled across the room. That was nothing that couldn't be fixed with a hammer and some nails in a couple of minutes, but it was further proof that there wasn't a man around here on a regular basis.

Maggie hurried back into the parlor with a cloth, a small brown bottle, and some sticking plaster. "Sit down on that sofa, and I'll play nurse," she ordered Longarm.

"I already washed out this cut, if that's what you're thinking—" he began.

"Did you clean it with anything besides water?"

"Well, no, but—"

Again she interrupted briskly. "Sit down. This won't take but a minute."

Longarm gave up and did as he was told. He sat on the claw-footed sofa Maggie had indicated, and she sank down on its cushions beside him. The cushions gave a little as she leaned toward him and started dabbing at the cut on his forehead with the cloth, which she had wet with the solution from the bottle. He recognized the tang of carbolic acid. The way she was sitting, her right thigh was pressed up against his left one, and even through their clothes he felt the warmth of her flesh.

He caught his breath as the carbolic stung the wound. Maggie said solemnly, "I know it burns, but this will keep the cut from becoming infected."

"Yes, ma'am," Longarm said. Some women liked to fuss over a fella when he was hurt, no matter how bad it really was or wasn't, and evidently Maggie Flynn was that sort. He sat there stolidly while she finished cleaning the wound, then attached a square of sticking plaster on it.

"There," she said as she sat back. Her leg was still mashed against his. "That wasn't too bad, was it?"

"Not bad at all," Longarm agreed, though he couldn't have said if he was talking about her medical attentions or the way her thigh was pressed up against his.

For a moment they sat there silently, looking at each other, and then Maggie looked down as Longarm cleared his throat. "I'd better put these things away," she said as she got to her feet. "Then we can get on with supper."

Longarm had already caught a whiff of what smelled like roast cooking. His mouth was beginning to water. He said, "That sounds fine to me."

"Come into the dining room."

He followed her out of the parlor, into the hall, and through an arched entrance into the dining room. The table was already set, and a laugh burst from Longarm's lips when he saw the half-full pitcher of lemonade and the two full glasses that had already been poured from it. "You must make mighty good lemonade, Miss Maggie," he said. "You're bound and determined that I give it a try."

"I still owe it to you from this afternoon. If we hadn't been so rudely interrupted . . ."

"No need to worry about that," Longarm told her. "Nobody's going to bother us tonight."

For a second, she looked as if she wanted to ask him how he could be so sure of that, but then she gave a little shrug of acceptance and said, "Sit down. I'll be right back."

Longarm sat, but then hopped right back up again when she returned from the kitchen with a platter containing a good-sized chunk of roast. It was surrounded by the potatoes and carrots with which it had been cooked. Longarm thought the food looked and smelled delicious, and he said as much.

Maggie blushed with pleasure. "I don't get to cook for anyone but myself most of the time," she said. "I may be out of practice."

"I seriously doubt that, ma'am."

"Please . . . just call me Maggie." She smiled at him. "I get ma'amed enough at school by the children."

"Sure, Maggie." Longarm held her chair for her as she sat down, then resumed his own seat.

The meal was every bit as good as Longarm had anticipated. The roast was tender and flavorful, the vegetables seasoned just right. And the lemonade was good, just sweet enough to keep its sharp bite from being overpowering. They made small talk as they ate, mostly about the students at Little Elm's school, who sounded from Maggie's tales about them as if they were as mischievous as little kids everywhere. Longarm enjoyed the conversation as much as he did the food, even more, and by the time dinner was over, he was relaxed and even a mite drowsy.

He thought about slipping one of his cheroots from his shirt pocket and firing it up, then decided against it. He was sure Maggie wouldn't have objected, but it just didn't seem right at the moment.

What would seem right, he realized as he watched her smiling while she related another story about her students, was leaning over and kissing her.

"I reckon I ought to be going," he said.

Maggie looked surprised. "So soon?"

"Well . . . I rode a ways today, so I'm a little tired."

"Oh. Of course." She took her napkin from her lap and placed it on the table next to her plate. "I shouldn't keep you from your rest."

Longarm stood up and held her chair for her as she got to her feet. "I'd be glad to help you clean up the table before I go," he offered.

"That's not necessary." She took a step closer to him, so close that she could have reached out and rested a hand on his chest if she had wanted to do so. Her head tilted back so she could look up at him. "There is one thing you can do before you go. . . ."

"Anything," Longarm said, and meant it.

She reached up, put her hand on the back of his neck, and came up on her toes as she drew his head down. Her lips met his in a kiss. Somehow, she must have been thinking the same thing he was a few moments earlier, Longarm realized.

The kiss started out gentle, but her mouth grew hotter and hungrier, and Longarm responded in kind. His arms went around her, drawing her to him and molding her body to his. He felt the press of her breasts against his chest. Her lips opened, and her tongue darted daringly into his mouth.

When they finally broke the kiss, Longarm wasn't the least bit drowsy anymore. In fact, he was wide awake. He was also hard as a rock, and Maggie had to be able to feel his arousal prodding against the softness of her belly. She didn't seem to mind.

Longarm looked down into her blue eyes and said, "I thought you claimed you weren't interested in romance, Maggie."

"I'm not," she said, "but I could surely use a good fucking right now, Custis. That is, if you're not too tired."

Longarm's mouth curved into a smile. Anything to oblige a lady, that was his rule.

And besides, she had fed him a mighty good supper.

Chapter 7

Maggie led him into her bedroom, and then began undressing him with an urgency that was mute testimony to the need she felt. She unbuttoned his shirt and spread it open, then caressed the muscular planes of his chest, sliding her fingers through the thick mat of dark brown hair that covered it. She peeled the shirt completely off him and tossed it into a corner. Her fingers went to the buckle of his gunbelt.

"Let me do that," Longarm said quietly. He took off the belt and holster and placed them on a small table beside the bed.

Deftly, Maggie unfastened the belt around his waist and unbuttoned the denim trousers. She slipped her hand inside and cupped the hard shaft through his long underwear for a moment before whispering, "Sit down. I'll take your boots off."

"I can do that," Longarm offered.

She put her hands on his shoulders. "No. I want to."

Longarm lowered himself to the edge of the bed. Maggie turned her back to him and bent over to grasp the booted right foot that he lifted. In the soft yellow glow of the lamp she'd lit, he had a good view of her rump in the blue dress. It was mighty appealing.

She pulled the right boot off, then the left, stripping Longarm's socks with them. When she turned around, he stood up again. She lowered his trousers so that he could step out of them and kick them aside. That left him clad only in the bottom half of a pair of long underwear. Maggie stepped closer and put her arms around his waist. She leaned her head down and fastened her lips around his left nipple as she slipped her hands in the back of the underwear. Her hands cupped his buttocks, digging hard into the muscular flesh, as she tongued the nipple.

Longarm was so hard he felt as if his shaft was about to rip an opening in the underwear. It was like busting free from prison when she finally peeled the garment down and released his manhood. To pull the underwear all the way down, she had to kneel in front of him, and he was acutely aware of how close the head of his organ was to her face.

So was she. She leaned a little closer and rubbed her cheek against the head. His shaft throbbed at the feel of Maggie's warm breath on it.

"He's beautiful," she murmured as she studied the impressive length and thickness of Longarm's shaft. She took hold of it with both hands, gripping it at the base and then sliding her palms along it toward her. A drop of moisture welled from the slit and pearled at the tip, and Maggie's tongue shot out to lick it off.

Longarm almost lost it then. It took a supreme effort of will to keep his climax from shooting out all over her lovely face. He gripped her shoulders and pulled her up, growling, "Let's get those clothes off of you."

He had undressed a lot of women in his life. His fingers moved with practiced ease over the buttons and stays of her clothing. The blue dress came off and flew into the corner along with his shirt. His thumbs slipped the straps of the chemise she wore under it off her shoulders. It dropped to her waist, leaving her breasts bare. They were pear-shaped, with nipples about the same size and color as a pair of new pennies. The little buds of flesh were hard and straining. Longarm bent his head and ran the tip of his tongue around the left one. A shiver went through Maggie's body.

"You lovely man," she whispered.

Longarm moved to the other nipple. Maggie put her hands on his head, stroking his hair as he opened his mouth wider and engulfed half of her breast. At the same time, he pushed the chemise and her petticoat down over her hips. With a single shimmy, she caused the silky undergarments to fall the rest of the way to the floor. All she had to do was step out of her slippers, and she was as naked as Longarm was.

He stepped back to look at her. She was truly lovely. Somehow, she managed to look both sensuous and innocent at the same time. He knew perfectly well she was no virgin; she had been married, after all. And her blue eyes shone with a lust that wasn't the least bit innocent as she studied his naked body with the same intensity he was affording hers.

Her curves were just about perfect, Longarm thought. His gaze slid down from her breasts to her softly rounded belly to the triangle of fine-spun hair at the juncture of her thighs. The hair was sandy-colored, a shade darker than the hair on her head. He stepped closer to her and reached down to stroke it, reveling in the softness of it for a moment before he cupped the mound which it covered. Her legs parted slightly as he squeezed. He moved his fingers farther and felt hot slickness against them.

She was more than ready for him. The folds of her femininity were drenched with moisture. She clutched his shaft and practically moaned, "Now, Custis. Please, now!"

She fell back on the bed and Longarm went with her. Her thighs opened, spreading wide in invitation. Longarm moved over her, his hips poised above hers. She still had hold of his manhood, and she guided the tip of it to her opening. Longarm felt the heat and the wetness against him, and with a surge of his hips he entered her, penetrating her

58

with a smooth thrust that left him buried deeply within her.

Maggie gasped and closed her eyes as Longarm filled her. He stayed where he was for a moment, holding himself still, letting her grow accustomed to the sensation of having so much male flesh lodged inside her body once again. Most of his weight was off her, supported on his elbows and knees, but he was pressing down on her hard enough so that her breasts were flattened against his chest. He could feel the erect nipples prodding him.

With a jerk, Maggie's hips began to pump hard. Her arms went around his neck and gripped him so tightly she seemed to be holding on for dear life. She cried out, driving her pelvis against his, then froze as spasms rippled through the tight sheath where he was buried. Her climax shook her for a long moment.

Longarm still hadn't moved. He waited as the seconds ticked by and Maggie's breathing slowed.

Then, flexing his hips, he drew back until only the head of his shaft was lodged within her. She whimpered.

He drove forward, filling her again, and her whimper turned into a frenzied "Oh!"

Longarm launched into a steady rhythm, sliding back and forth inside her. He kissed her, his tongue spearing deep into her mouth, penetrating her there just as surely as his manhood was driving into her core down below. As his pace increased, she tore her mouth away from his and panted, "Oh, yes! Yes! Do it to me!"

Somehow, Longarm held back his climax until a fine sheen of sweat covered both of them and Maggie had exploded a couple more times. She pulled her knees back as far as they would go and looped her calves over his shoulders, so that he could delve deeper into her than ever before. She caught hold of his buttocks again and pulled hard on them, as if she was trying to urge him even deeper. "So full, so full," she whispered raggedly.

Longarm felt his climax boiling up and knew there was nothing he could do to stop it this time. He drove into her again, so that he could feel the head of his shaft touching her innermost core, and froze that way as he began to erupt. Maggie screamed as spurt after spurt of his thick, scalding seed filled her.

Finally, as the spasms that shook both of them began to die away, Longarm started to ease his weight off Maggie. She clutched at him and said hoarsely, "No. Please, stay right . . . right where you are . . . for a minute. It's been so long. . . ."

Longarm stayed where he was. He raised a hand and stroked her cheek, then cupped her chin and kissed her. Maggie hugged him tightly and sighed.

"All right," she whispered. "Thank you, Custis. You gave me just what I needed."

Longarm rolled off her and then slipped an arm underneath her shoulders, pulling her to him. She rolled onto her side and nestled against him. They lay there contentedly like that for several minutes, catching their breath and allowing their heart rates to slow to something more closely approaching normal.

"Stay here tonight," Maggie suggested.

Longarm frowned. "Don't know if that would be good for your reputation," he said.

"To hell with my reputation. I never had that much of one after Tim went to prison anyway."

Longarm didn't want to stir up any bad memories in her, so he nodded. "All right," he said. "I'll stay." He supposed nobody at the Thorne House would care whether he slept in the room he had rented or not.

The hotel room window went up soundlessly. It had been oiled recently so that it could be opened without making a lot of noise. The dark figure that had come creeping along the narrow balcony on the front of the hotel knew that.

It was the middle of the night. Little Elm's main street was deserted. The Horsehead Saloon and Casey's Bar were both still open, but by this hour of the morning, the drinkers

60

in those two establishments weren't interested in anything except the contents of their glasses. Whenever one of them did stagger out and start stumbling toward home, none of them looked up at the Thorne House balcony.

The figure swung a leg over the windowsill and stepped quietly into the room, brushing the curtains aside. Moving with sure, silent steps, the intruder crossed the short distance to the bed.

The stranger's saddlebags were lying on the covers. The intruder reached down and picked them up, opening them and sliding a hand inside each of the pouches in turn. One of the saddlebags contained a couple of spare shirts, an extra set of long underwear, and an oilcloth slicker that had been rolled into a tight cylinder. In the other pouch were a box of cartridges—.44's, almost surely—as well as a small wooden chest filled with cheroots. A silver flask and a canteen were in the bottom of the saddlebag. A stray beam of moonlight that filtered through the window glinted dully on the metal surface of the flask.

The intruder determined all of that by groping through the saddlebags. When everything had been put back as before, the shadowy figure replaced the bags on the bed, putting them down in as close to their original positions as possible. Soundlessly, the shape crossed the room again, this time going to the corner where Longarm had left his Winchester. There was nothing unusual about the weapon, the intruder decided after examining it, again working by feel in the dark.

Returning to the bed, the intruder knelt beside it. An arm reached underneath the bed, the hand searching for anything that didn't belong there. The questing fingers encountered nothing but a couple of balls of dust.

There was nowhere else to hide anything in the room. With a sigh, the intruder came to that conclusion. This nocturnal visit to the stranger's room wasn't going to pay any dividends after all. The stranger wasn't even here, so he couldn't be killed and disposed of. Not yet anyway.

The shadowy figure departed the same way it had come, little more than a moving patch of deeper darkness as it slipped out the window and lowered the glass. Chances were, the stranger would never even know that someone had been in his room tonight.

The intruder was disappointed, but not too much. If the stranger was really a threat, there would be other chances to tend to the matter.

Other chances to kill.

Longarm woke with Maggie cuddled against his back. He was lying on his right side, having slept soundly. He felt her warm breath against the back of his neck as she kissed him there. Her hand slid along his flank. Both of them were still naked, and the sensation of bare flesh against bare flesh was mighty pleasant.

It was also enough to make him begin to harden. His shaft gave a little jump, and became even more rigid as she parted the cheeks of his rump and explored the crevice between them.

He started to roll toward her, but she stopped him with a whispered, "No. Stay there. Let me."

Longarm did as he was told and stayed where he was, his heart hammering and his breath coming faster as her touch grew even bolder. After a few moments, she reached between his thighs and cupped the heavy sacs that lay below his erect manhood. Her fingers were gentle and maddeningly sensuous.

Her hand went away, and she breathed, "Now, roll on your back."

She moved around on the bed as Longarm did so. His shaft stood straight and tall as Maggie threw the covers back. She came up on her knees and leaned over him. Silky strands of her blond hair brushed his organ and drew a groan from him. She took hold of him with both hands and lowered her mouth to the head of his shaft, kissing it lightly for a moment before opening her lips and taking it inside.

Longarm closed his eyes and gave himself over to the sheer pleasure Maggie was bestowing on him. Her lips moved lower and lower on the thick pole of male flesh as she swallowed more and more of him. He felt as if the entire essence of his being was concentrated there, and that she was taking all of him into the warm, wet cavern of her mouth.

It went away, leaving him feeling lost and disoriented for a second, and Maggie said, "Watch me."

Longarm lifted his head and opened his eyes. "What?"

"Prop the pillows behind your head so you can watch me." She smiled wickedly at him.

Longarm grinned as he realized what she meant. He levered himself up in the bed and stuffed both pillows behind his head and shoulders. From this position he had a good view as she knelt beside him and leaned over his groin again. A growl rumbled up from deep inside him as she resumed sucking him.

She made a mighty pretty picture with her blond hair tousled from sleep and her mouth full of his manhood. He reached down lazily to toy with her right breast, the only one he could reach at the moment. After a while he slid his hand on down her side to her hip and slipped it underneath her, finding her wet center and probing it with a finger.

A gasp came from her as she took her mouth off his shaft again. "Later," she said breathlessly. "There'll be plenty of time for me. This time is for you."

Longarm wasn't going to argue. Gray light came in through the gauzy curtains over Maggie's bedroom window, so he knew it wasn't too late in the morning. As she'd said, there would be time. . . .

He lay there and watched as she drenched his shaft, slathering it from tip to base with her tongue and lightly nipping it occasionally with her teeth. She popped each of his sacs into her mouth and gently sucked on them in turn, then began gradually swallowing his manhood once more. Longarm's hips wanted to arch up off the bed, but he suppressed the impulse so that he wouldn't gag her. She slipped a hand underneath him and sought out the muscles of his rump, kneading and squeezing them.

Finally, in a hoarse voice, Longarm said, "I ain't going to be able to hold off much longer, Maggie."

Her mouth glided off him for a second and she said, "That's all right. I want it." Then she engulfed him again.

Longarm couldn't have stopped it now. He groaned as he lifted his hips from the bed and began emptying himself in her mouth.

Maggie moaned in passion too as she sought to take what he was giving her. The muscles of her throat worked as she swallowed. She clutched at him and shuddered, and though he was too far gone to pay much attention to it at the time, he realized later that she was in the throes of her own culmination.

Eventually, Longarm fell back on the bed, totally drained. He didn't feel that he would be able to stand up for a week, let alone make love again to Maggie or accomplish anything else.

But he had always been a pretty resilient cuss, he reminded himself. Give him time to catch his breath, and there was no telling what he could do, he thought.

Maggie threw herself down beside him. "That was wonderful," she said. "I used to wake up Tim that way."

The comment surprised Longarm a little, but if Maggie didn't mind talking about her late husband at a moment like this, that was her business. He said, "Ol' Tim must've woke up happy a lot then."

"I hope so. I . . . I wish I'd been able to make him even happier. If I had, he might not have gotten mixed up with that gang of bank robbers. He might not have ever learned how to make nitroglycerine."

Longarm lifted his head. "Nitro . . . glycerine?"

Maggie pushed back a strand of hair that had fallen in her face. "Yes. It's the explosive that's found in dynamite.

64

But in its purest form, it's much more powerful than regular dynamite."

Longarm knew what nitroglycerine was. But he hadn't known until now that Timothy Flynn had been an expert with the stuff.

And Flynn's widow lived in a town that had nearly gotten itself blown clean off the map. . . .

Chapter 8

That thought percolated around in Longarm's brain for only a few seconds before he gave a mental shake of his head and discarded it. It was crazy to think that Maggie might have had anything to do with the raid on Little Elm and the devastation that had resulted. For one thing, she was a woman. For another, she lived here, taught school here. She wouldn't try to destroy her own home, would she?

Longarm knew from experience that gals were sometimes pretty talkative after they'd made love. Maggie seemed to be that sort, and since she had brought up her late husband, Longarm didn't think it would do any harm to try to find out more about him and his bank-robbing activities.

"Tell me about Tim," he said. "If you don't mind talking about him, that is."

"No, I don't," Maggie replied. "Somehow, this morning it seems all right. He was from Nebraska and came down here to Kansas to work in the stockyards at the railhead. We met in Hays City. I was on my way to Little Elm from St. Louis. I'd already accepted the job of schoolteacher here. Tim was . . . taken with me, I suppose you'd say."

"I can see why," Longarm said.

She blushed prettily. "Flatterer. You've got some blarney in you too, don't you?"

"I reckon. Some of my kin came over from Ireland a few generations back." Longarm paused, then asked, "Did Tim follow you here to Little Elm?"

"That's exactly what happened. He gave up his job in Hays and came here to be with me. We were married a month later."

"What did he do? Take up farming?"

Maggie made a face and shook her head. "He was raised on a farm in Nebraska and hated it. Said he'd never grub in the dirt again. So he tried to find work as a cowhand on the ranches west of here."

"Holcomb's Circle H?"

"No, Tim never rode for the Circle H. It would have made things even more awkward if he had, though it's hard to see how they could be worse where Brad is concerned."

"With any luck, he won't bother you again," Longarm said, but he didn't really believe that. Holcomb might stay away while Longarm was around, but sooner or later, Longarm would have to go back to Denver. Besides, Holcomb was arrogant and stubborn enough so that even Longarm's presence might not be enough to make him think twice about starting more trouble.

"Tim was never much good as a cowhand either. The town allowed me to continue teaching after we were married, but my wages weren't enough for us to live on. He did some odd jobs around town, like that man Rory Pierce who was probably killed in the explosions, but that didn't bring in much." Maggie shook her head sadly. "Tim was such a proud man, and so upset that he wasn't providing for me the way he thought he should. I suppose when he met Simon it was inevitable that nothing good would come of it."

"Simon?" Longarm repeated.

"Simon Dugan. Tim met him in Casey's Bar. Fellow Irishman, you know. Simon was a drifter and a gambler, but what he really fancied himself as was a bad man. He was forming a gang to rob banks, and once Tim fell in with them . . ." Maggie looked down and sighed.

"Your husband told you all about this?" Longarm hoped she wouldn't think he was too curious.

"That's right. Tim didn't believe in keeping secrets from me." Maggie laughed softly, but there was no humor in the sound. "Sometimes I wish he had. I could have been happier, longer, in my ignorance."

Longarm didn't prod her when she fell silent this time, and in a moment, she resumed the story.

"They started by hitting a bank north of here, in a little town just over the border in Nebraska. There were six of them, counting Tim, and everything went smoothly. No one was hurt, Tim said. Nobody even fired a gun. That encouraged them, and they robbed two more banks, back here in Kansas."

"You knew about all this?"

"Yes."

"And you didn't tell the law?"

Maggie sat up straighter, and her chin lifted in defiance. Her eyes flashed as she said, "Don't you judge me. He was my husband, and I loved him with all my heart. Of course I didn't tell the authorities."

Longarm held up his hands, palms out. "Hold on. I didn't mean for that to sound the way it did." Although in truth, the comment had been startled out of him and was genuine. "I don't have much of a soft spot for the law myself," he lied. "I'd have done just the same as you did."

That seemed to mollify Maggie. She said, "I didn't approve, mind you. I tried to get Tim to stop. I begged him. It didn't do any good. He had failed at nearly everything he'd tried in his life, he said, and now he was successful at *something,* even if it was illegal.

"But then they ran into a bank with a safe that was too strong for them to bust open. Simon suggested that in the future they use dynamite in those situations, but Tim had read somewhere about nitroglycerine and he decided he'd learn how to make it."

"Boil it off dynamite, don't you?" Longarm asked.

Maggie nodded. "That's the simplest way, Tim said. But it's dangerous. The stuff can explode while you're extracting it, and once you have some, it's still very unstable. A hard jolt can easily cause it to explode."

"Sounds like a nasty business," Longarm commented with a shake of his head.

"Yes, nasty and dangerous." She smiled. "But the gang was able to blow open every safe they ran into after that."

"Your husband sounds like a smart man. How'd he get caught?"

"Too smart for his own good," Maggie said ruefully. "He bought the dynamite openly, going from town to town in this end of Kansas and picking up some in every place he came to, thinking that no one would ever put it together what he was using it for. Eventually the law traced his movements that way and followed him back here. They arrested him, and Tim never denied what he had done. In a strange way, I think he was even proud of it."

"What about Dugan and the others?"

Maggie shook her head. "I have no idea where they are. They weren't with Tim when he was arrested, and he was much too proud to reveal their identities to the authorities. I suppose they heard about his arrest and left Kansas."

Longarm frowned. "And it doesn't bother you that they got away scot-free while your husband was sent to prison? They were just as guilty as he was."

"Perhaps even more guilty, since it was all Simon's idea to start robbing banks in the first place. But it wasn't their fault Tim was caught. I can't hold what happened to him against them."

"Well, you're a heap more generous than I would be under those circumstances," Longarm told her.

"What could I do? Inform on them? Tell the sheriff that they were in on the robberies with Tim?"

"It's a thought," Longarm said.

She shook her head. "Tim wouldn't do that when he had the chance to. I won't either."

She was sure as hell a strange one, Longarm thought. Not at all the simple, pretty schoolmarm she seemed at first glance.

"You're telling *me* about it," Longarm pointed out.

"You're not a lawman. What *are* you? You never told me your line of work."

Longarm decided to continue the masquerade he had begun with Sheriff Kingman and Carl Thorne. "I'm a journalist. I write for a magazine back East."

Maggie clapped a hand to her mouth in surprise and alarm. "Oh, my! You won't write about what I told you, will you, Custis? Please, I thought I was speaking in confidence—"

"Don't worry," Longarm interrupted. "I promise I'll never write a magazine story about anything you said." That was true too. The most he'd write up would be a report for Billy Vail.

Maggie lowered her hand to her breast and heaved a sigh of relief. "Thank you, Custis. I knew you were an . . . an honorable man. I knew it just by talking to you. If I didn't think you could be trusted, I'd never have asked you to spend the night." She moved closer to him on the bed and reached over to fondle his organ, which was flaccid at the moment. Under her touch, however, it began to grow. She whispered, "I'm glad I asked you."

There was still more Longarm wanted to know, but the way she was playing with him was mighty distracting. The rest of his questions would have to wait, he decided.

When Longarm was fully erect again, Maggie moved to the edge of the bed and positioned herself there on her hands and knees. Her pretty rump was sticking up in the air, cheeks spread to reveal the puckered brown ring and the enticing pink slit below it. As Longarm stood up from the bed and moved behind her, she said in a throaty voice, "Take your pick."

"Well, I've never been greedy. . . ." Longarm said.

"Indulge yourself," Maggie invited.

So that was exactly what Longarm did.

Later Maggie fixed breakfast, and Longarm sat at the kitchen table as she placed a plate full of hotcakes, bacon, fried potatoes, and fried eggs in front of him. She poured a cup of coffee that smelled wonderful, and gave that to him as well. He sipped the hot, strong brew and gave a sigh of satisfaction. "A fella could get used to treatment like this," he said.

Maggie looked pretty as a picture in a housedress with little flowers all over it. Her blond hair was pulled back and tied behind her head. Looking like that, she could have almost passed for a young girl . . . if Longarm hadn't been aware of the lusty, complex woman she really was.

She sat down across from him with her own food and coffee and asked, "How long do you plan to stay in Little Elm?" She added quickly, "I'm not trying to pin you down or anything. I know how you men hate that."

"Not always," Longarm said. "Sometimes we don't mind being pinned down at all." He gave her a mock lecherous grin and wiggled his eyebrows, which made her laugh and blush prettily at the same time.

"You know what I mean."

He grew more serious. "Yeah, I reckon I do. Truth is, I haven't given it much thought. I was just passing through when I saw what had happened here and decided to stick around for a few days to find out more about it. Thought there might be a good story in it." He frowned slightly. "Did it ever occur to you that there are some similarities between what happened here and the bank robberies your husband's gang used to pull?"

Maggie looked shocked. "It wasn't Tim's gang. Simon Dugan was the leader."

71

"Tim handled the explosives for them, though, and . . . well, you saw for yourself what happened here in Little Elm."

"The explosions and the fires, you mean."

Longarm shrugged, the gesture and his silence eloquent in their meaning.

Maggie gnawed for a moment on her lower lip. Both she and Longarm had forgotten for the time being about breakfast. The silence stretched out uncomfortably, and finally she sighed.

"From what I've seen and heard, the explosions *were* quite powerful. They could have been caused by nitroglycerine."

"Did anybody else in Dugan's gang handle the stuff besides your husband?"

She shook her head. "They were all afraid of it. Regular dynamite is unstable and dangerous enough, but nitroglycerine is even worse."

"Maybe Dugan found himself somebody else who ain't afraid of it," Longarm suggested.

"I suppose it's possible. . . ."

"Dugan would know there was a bank here in Little Elm, wouldn't he?"

Maggie nodded. "Yes, and he would know when to hit it so that several of the ranches would have their payrolls on hand at the time of the raid."

That angle was new to Longarm; no one had said anything to him so far about payrolls. "Is that what happened?"

"I think so. You'd have to ask Sheriff Kingman or Mr. Carruthers, the president of the bank, to be sure."

Longarm nodded slowly, his brow furrowed in thought, and Maggie looked at him intently. She said, "You *are* thinking about writing about this, aren't you?"

"You've got to admit, it's a pretty interesting story," Longarm said. If he really had been a journalist, he might have been tempted to write it up.

"Yes, I suppose it is. I've been thinking, Custis. Maybe

I was wrong to make you promise not to use the story." She leaned forward, becoming more eager as she went on. "If you told the truth about things, it wouldn't clear Tim's name, of course, since he *was* guilty, but it might make people see him in a little different light. Maybe they would see that he wasn't really so bad. At least while he was riding with the gang, no one was killed."

"Maybe you're right," Longarm allowed. "I admit, I want to look into the raid here at Little Elm and try to find out who was responsible for it. If it was Dugan's bunch, how would you feel about that?"

Maggie took a deep breath. "If Simon and the other men were the ones who robbed the bank here, then so be it. I never liked them, never wanted Tim to be one of them."

Longarm nodded. "I'll poke around a mite then, see what I can find out."

"Good. Because . . . I'm not ready for you to leave town yet," Maggie said. "Can I admit that I'd like for you to stay around for a while without frightening you off?"

"You can tell me anything you want," Longarm said with a grin, "as long as you keep fixing meals like this one."

"And doing what we did last night?"

"And doing what we did last night," Longarm agreed.

She blushed again. "You must think I'm a terrible hussy."

"Nope. Just a woman who needed some loving."

"I still do." Maggie's eyes shone as she added, "Hurry up and finish that breakfast, Custis. I have other plans for you."

Longarm liked the sound of that.

Chapter 9

Longarm managed to get out of Maggie's house before she completely wore him out. He left by the back way so he wouldn't do any more damage to her reputation than had already been done by her late husband and his bank-robbing ways. Longarm was a little surprised that the townspeople of Little Elm would tolerate the widow of a jailbird teaching their children in school, but he knew it wasn't always easy to get qualified teachers out in the West. Besides, even though some folks snubbed Maggie, they had to know that what Timothy Flynn had done had not been her fault.

Longarm went along the alley to the rear entrance of the Thorne House and up the stairs to his room. A glance at the narrow gap between the jamb and the door told him the matchstick he had placed there the previous evening was still where it was supposed to be. He was careful anyway as he unlocked the door and stepped into the room. Someone could have come in through the window and been waiting for him. Longarm didn't move his hand away from the butt of his gun until he saw that the room was empty.

He had shaved and washed his face at Maggie's house before leaving there. Now he changed shirts and went downstairs again, this time going through the lobby. Carl Thorne was once again behind the desk. The hotel owner had been on duty every time Longarm had seen him. Thorne greeted him with a friendly smile and said, "Morning, Mr. Polk. Sleep well?"

"Fine," Longarm said. He was going to have to tell Maggie about how he had used the Polk name with Thorne and Sheriff Kingman. She believed him to be a journalist, so she ought to believe him about the false name too. That would simplify matters.

"Going over to the hash house for breakfast?" Thorne asked.

Longarm couldn't very well tell the man that he had already eaten his fill at Maggie Flynn's kitchen table. Instead he said, "I'm not really hungry this morning. Thought I might take a ride instead."

"I'm afraid there's not much to see around here. This isn't the most scenic part of the world."

"Doesn't take much to interest me," Longarm said.

"Well, then, I hope you enjoy yourself."

Longarm left the hotel by the front entrance so he could get a look at what was going on up and down the main street. The reconstruction efforts were under way again for the day, and wagons were parked in front of the stores that had survived the explosions and fire. It might be a mistake to say that Little Elm was bustling, but its business was coming back.

Most importantly, Longarm didn't see any sign of Brad Holcomb or his riders. Holcomb and his men must have gone back out to the Circle H after the fracas the day before and stayed there.

Longarm circled around to the rear of the hotel and went into the corral to saddle his horse. He led the bay out, shut the gate, and swung up on the animal's back. Heeling the horse into a trot, he rode southwest out of town, toward the low hills in the distance. According to everything he had heard, the bank robbers had fled in that direction, and it was in the rocky hills that the belated posse led by Sheriff Kingman had lost the trail.

Before leaving Maggie's, Longarm had asked her if her husband had ever said anything about where the gang's hideout was located. She had shaken her head and explained that Timothy Flynn had always rendezvoused with Dugan and the others somewhere outside of Little Elm whenever they were going to pull a job. She hadn't known where the meeting place was, and to tell the truth, she hadn't wanted to know, she told Longarm. The less she knew about her husband's illegal activities, the easier it was to pretend to herself that nothing was going on.

Longarm reached the hills at mid-morning and spent several hours riding through them seemingly aimlessly. He hadn't bothered watching for tracks during the ride out from Little Elm, since too much time had passed since the night of the robbery. Anyway, the posse's mounts had probably obliterated most of the hoofprints left by the gang's horses. Once he was in the hills, however, he kept a closer eye out for any sign of riders. This was pretty isolated country, too rocky for farming and too sparse in vegetation to make good grazing land. Men who were on the move out here were probably bound on other errands . . . nefarious, bloody-handed errands, as E. E. Polk might phrase it, Longarm thought with a grin.

He ran across a few tracks, but he wasn't able to follow any of them for more than a few miles before they petered out. Nor did he see any telltale tendrils of smoke in the sky that might have marked the location of a hidden camp. Feeling frustrated along toward the middle of the afternoon, Longarm swung his horse to the south and rode out of the range of hills. He kept his mount's nose pointed in the same direction until he reached the railroad tracks. Then he turned east and followed the rails to the flag stop where he had left the train the day before.

There was a telegraph office there, and Longarm quickly composed a message to Billy Vail, explaining to the chief marshal that he was posing as Edward Ezekiel Polk while he investigated the explosions and bank robbery at Little

Elm. Billy would probably get a chuckle out of that, seeing as how it was Longarm's desire to get away from Polk that had gotten him involved in this case in the first place. Longarm concluded the telegram:

CONTACT ME AS POLK AT THORNE HOUSE LITTLE ELM
STOP

There was a Western Union office in Little Elm too, and now Vail would have a way to get in touch with him without revealing who Longarm really was.

That done, he paid the operator, left the flag stop, and headed north again on the bay gelding. He had ridden in a big circle today and had nothing to show for it.

Longarm supposed he wasn't really paying attention as the horse jogged steadily northward. He was tired and hungry and frustrated, and he had already started thinking about Maggie Flynn and what delights, culinary and otherwise, might await him at her house tonight. So he wasn't really expecting trouble.

Luckily his instincts took over when he spotted a flash of red from a thicket of trees up ahead. Warning bells went off, and the realization that the flash was likely the setting sun glinting off metal sent him rolling out of the saddle and pitching headlong to the ground. At the same instant, a rifle cracked spitefully, and the bay gave a startled leap as a bullet creased its shoulder. The horse whinnied shrilly in pain.

Longarm was moving even as he landed heavily on the ground. He rolled over and came up on his toes, springing toward the nearest cover, which was a small mound of earth to the side of the trail. The top of the mound was covered with wildflowers. One of them jerked and fell over, its stem cut by a second bullet. Longarm heard the shot as he sprawled on his belly behind the mound.

He heard galloping hoofbeats and bit back a curse as he

looked over to see the bay stampeding away down the road. Bushwhacked, set afoot, and pinned down behind this pile of dirt. Could things get any worse? Longarm wondered..

A bullet struck the ground beside his head and kicked grit in his eyes. That was his answer, he supposed. There were more than one of the bastards, and they had him in a cross fire.

There was a gully about fifteen feet to his right. That was the logical shelter he would try to reach. He rolled in that direction, then reversed course abruptly as another bullet plowed into the ground near him. His first move had been only a feint. He lunged to his feet and broke into a run that carried him back across the trail. Both of the bushwhackers had likely expected him to go the other direction, and it took them a second to correct their aims. Longarm heard a bullet whine past, but it was behind him.

He threw himself forward in a dive that carried him into some tall grass. When he landed, the ground fell away unexpectedly beneath him. He slid down the slope and at its bottom splashed into a narrow stream that he hadn't even known was there. The tall grass had concealed it. The trickle wasn't more than a foot wide at the moment, but it had carved out a furrow that was several feet deep as it meandered across the prairie. Longarm stretched out in it and drew his gun.

The Colt was a little damp, but Longarm felt confident it would fire just fine. He waited there, motionless, his clothes growing soaked from the flow of the little stream. In early summer like this, the water wasn't particularly cold, but Longarm started to grow chilled anyway. He grimaced in anger at the bushwhackers.

At the same time, the wheels of his brain were clicking over rapidly. Who had reason to want him dead? Brad Holcomb maybe. The rancher could have had a man watching him, could have easily set up this ambush to get rid of a man he saw as a rival for Maggie Flynn. But Maggie had said that Holcomb wasn't the type to do that, and Longarm

78

had felt the same way about him. Holcomb was an arrogant, stubborn son of a bitch, to be sure, but Longarm didn't think he was a cold-blooded killer.

Bandits were always a possibility. More than one solitary traveler had been bushwhacked for whatever valuables he might have been carrying.

Or maybe somebody didn't like the fact that he was poking around Little Elm and trying to find out exactly what had happened there. He had told Kingman and Thorne that he was a writer, and there was no way of knowing at the moment who else they might have told. If someone in Little Elm had a connection to the gang of bank robbers, they could have seen him ride out today, could have followed him into the hills and realized he was searching for the gang's hideout. . . .

Longarm muttered a curse as he realized that pretending to be a writer might be every bit as dangerous as revealing that he was really a lawman. Well, it had seemed like a good idea at the time, he thought, and it had appealed to his sense of the ironic. Live and learn, he told himself.

Or, if he was damned unlucky, die and learn.

The sound of horses walking somewhere nearby made him lift his head. Either someone else was riding along the trail, unaware of what had happened here, or else the bushwhackers were searching for him. A moment later, a harsh voice spoke and settled that question.

"Be careful. That bastard crawled in here somewheres."

Another voice said, "It's like lookin' for a snake in all this tall grass. Damned if I like it."

Longarm didn't recognize either of the voices. The men were strangers to him, which lent credence to his bandit theory, but they could still be connected somehow with the bank robbers.

"I don't care if you like it or not. Just find him so we can make sure he's dead."

"Dead, hell! I don't think we even hit him."

"I hit him, all right," the first voice insisted. "I saw the

79

son of a bitch jump. He's hit bad, I reckon."

They were right above him now, moving along the bank of the little stream and using the barrels of their rifles to poke through the grass. Longarm waited a heartbeat, lying utterly still as they moved past him. Then he pushed himself up and grated, "You reckon wrong, mister."

The two men spun toward him, one of them yelping in surprise while the other cursed under his breath. Longarm fired before the rifle barrels could swing completely around. His first bullet smacked into the chest of one of the men, knocking him backward. Longarm aimed for the shoulder of the second man, intending to take him alive. The bullet just clipped the man's right shoulder, however, staggering him but not putting him down. What Longarm had not noticed right away was that the bushwhacker was left-handed and still had that hand wrapped around the stock of the Winchester he held. The man jerked the rifle up to fire it one-handed.

Longarm threw himself to the side and fired again as the rifle blasted practically in his face. The slug from the Winchester whipped past his ear. Longarm's hurriedly aimed bullet buried itself in the bushwhacker's belly, doubling the man over.

With a heartfelt "Damn it!" Longarm scrambled to his feet and hurried over to where the second bushwhacker had collapsed. He cast a glance at the other man, saw that his shot had punched neatly through the man's breast pocket, and knew that one was dead. Longarm kicked away the fallen rifle and then knelt at the side of the man who was still alive.

But not for long. The lower half of the man's shirt front was already soaked from the blood welling between the fingers that were clutching his stomach. His mouth opened and closed spasmodically, and his eyes were wide and staring with agony.

Longarm had never seen either man before.

He said urgently, "Listen to me. You're hit bad. I'll help

80

you, but you got to tell me why you tried to ambush me."

"Go to . . . hell . . ." the man rasped.

"You're going to be a long time dying, friend," Longarm lied. "Did Brad Holcomb send you after me? Was it Holcomb?"

There wasn't even a flicker of recognition in the man's eyes at Holcomb's name. Longarm tried another tack. He said, "I didn't think so. It was Dugan, wasn't it?"

It was a long shot, but it paid off. The man gasped, "How . . . how did you . . ."

Then his eyes glazed over and his head fell back, but it was enough. His reaction had told Longarm that the man knew Dugan's name.

That meant there was a strong possibility that Dugan and his old gang were operating again in this area. They had hit Little Elm, even though they were without the services of the late Timothy Flynn. Clearly, they had found another explosives expert.

Longarm straightened, grimacing at the way his soaked clothes stuck to his body. He holstered his gun and left the bodies where they had fallen. As far as he was concerned, the coyotes and the buzzards could have them. That was a suitable fate for bushwhackers, even would-be ones.

The men had left their horses at the side of the trail with their reins dangling. Longarm caught first one, then the other of the animals. Riding one and leading the other, he headed toward Little Elm again, and as he had hoped, he found his rented bay a couple of miles up the trail, peacefully cropping grass. The gelding had calmed down, and allowed Longarm to catch it without any trouble.

He turned the other two horses loose. Taking them into Little Elm would only lead to questions he didn't want to answer at the moment. Someone in the settlement was connected to Dugan and the other bank robbers. That was the only explanation for the attempt on Longarm's life.

His clothes were only partially dry by the time he got to town. He unsaddled the bay and left it in the corral, then

81

went upstairs and changed. Darkness had settled down over the community by the time he came downstairs again, once more leaving through the back door of the hotel without seeing the talkative Carl Thorne. Longarm had some questions for the hotel owner, most importantly who Thorne had told about "E. E. Polk," but that could wait. On the ride in, he had started to worry about Maggie. If Dugan's gang wanted to get rid of him, they might strike at Maggie too, fearful of what she might have told him about them.

He went straight to the rear door of her house, frowning as he noticed that the windows were dark. No one answered his soft knock. He waited a moment, knocked again with the same lack of results, then tried the doorknob. It turned easily.

Longarm drew his gun as he stepped inside. "Maggie?" he called. He was in the kitchen, he recalled, so he moved quietly toward the hall that led to the front of the house, past the dining room and the parlor on one side and Maggie's bedroom on the other. "Maggie?" he said again.

The hushed silence in the house told Longarm a story he didn't want to hear. After a moment, he fished a lucifer out of his shirt pocket and struck it with his thumbnail. As the match flared, Longarm squinted against its glare.

No sign of life met his narrowed eyes. He found a lamp, lit it, and carried it from room to room. All of them were empty except for the furniture. Nothing seemed to be out of place, no chairs overturned, no other signs of a disturbance or a struggle.

But Maggie Flynn was gone.

Chapter 10

The locomotive's headlight lanced out in front of it through the darkness, illuminating the tracks ahead of the bellowing iron behemoth. This stretch of railroad was flat and straight, and Carney Wilkes, the engineer, had a tendency of pushing the train to its highest speed along here, even when he was making the run at night. A big moon floated over the Kansas prairie. Even if the train hadn't had the headlight, Wilkes was confident he would be able to see well enough to spot any possible trouble up ahead.

"So then my wife's sister crawled in bed with us," Ben Granger, the fireman, shouted over the roar of the engine and the clatter of the wheels on the rails. "Whoo-eee! You ever romped with two gals at once, Carney? Ain't nothin' else like it in the world."

Wilkes shook his head, barely paying attention to Granger's lewd story. Granger always had some such yarn to spin. To hear the fireman tell it, he had bedded practically half the women between Kansas City and Denver, which was the regular run for him and Wilkes. Young women, old women, married women, widows, it didn't matter to Granger. If it was female, he'd dip his wick into it. Wilkes figured at least ninety percent of what Granger said was pure horseshit.

"Better stoke her a little," Wilkes said as he eyed the gauges above the throttle. Granger stopped yammering for a minute and opened the door of the firebox with one thickly gloved hand. He threw several shovelfuls of coal from the tender into the flames and then closed the door. The needles on the gauges crept up several marks, and Wilkes nodded in satisfaction.

"That's more like it," he said.

"You like to go fast, don't you, Carney?" Granger asked. "Lickety-split across these plains."

"We've got a schedule to keep," Wilkes growled. He understood that, even if Granger didn't comprehend much of anything that occurred above his own belt buckle.

"I know, I know. Got to make Denver by mornin'."

Granger just didn't understand how much folks depended on the railroad, Wilkes thought. The people dozing fitfully in the two passenger cars had places to go and things to do. Other people were waiting for the freight being carried in the boxcars. The locomotive was even pulling a special boxcar this trip, doing a job for the United States government. Nobody knew about that except Wilkes and old Ollie Thurston, the conductor. . . .

A mile ahead of the locomotive, out of reach of the train's headlight, a figure knelt beside the tracks. Deft fingers carefully placed a glass container in the angle formed by one of the tracks and a cross-tie. A short length of cord fastened it in place. The figure backed off, straightening to its full height, and started to breathe again.

"That ought to do it," a voice called softly as the dark shape turned toward its companions. Half a dozen figures on horseback loomed nearby.

"All right, let's go," one of the riders grated. The train's headlight was visible to the east, racing steadily closer. It had first come into sight several minutes earlier when the train was still miles away. A tiny, winking dot had grown into the inexorable cone of light that was even now fast approaching.

The steel rails began to hum as the vibrations going through them grew stronger. The riders kicked their horses into a gallop that carried them away from the tracks, heading north along a route perpendicular to the railroad.

The liquid in the glass container began to shake as the rail vibrated.

In the locomotive's cab, Carney Wilkes leaned out the window. His eyes narrowed, partially in response to the wind in his face and partially in suspicion. He thought he had seen something moving to the north of the tracks, a blur of motion in the darkness that might have been nothing more than a trick of the night shadows. But Wilkes's instincts warned him it was more than that.

Suddenly, with a flash so bright it was blinding, an explosion ripped through the night. The blast took place scarcely a dozen yards in front of the onrushing locomotive, gouging out a huge hole in the roadbed, throwing cross-ties high in the air, and twisting and bending the steel rails as if they were nothing more than straw. Even though Wilkes's reflexes and years of experience sent his hand leaping to the brake lever, there was nothing he could do. The locomotive's wheels hit the ripped-up section of track less than a heartbeat after the explosion.

For a second, the locomotive appeared to be trying to take flight like some huge, ungainly bird. Its front end came completely off the tracks, the cowcatcher pointing up toward the stars for a second instead of straight ahead. Then it crashed back to earth, slamming down on the sloping embankment beside the tracks and tearing long, deep furrows in the ground with its massive weight. The locomotive began to tip over.

Once that started, it was gone. The locomotive fell on its side, skidding along and plowing even deeper into the ground before it shuddered to a halt. The boiler burst, flooding the cab with scalding water. The water cooked the torn flesh of Carney Wilkes and Ben Granger, but neither man felt it. They were both already dead, Wilkes's neck broken and Granger crushed by the weight of the coal that had come crashing forward out of the tender as the locomotive lurched to its sudden, violent stop.

Behind the locomotive and the tender, the other cars followed their lead, leaping off the tracks and flying helter-skelter through the air for a second before coming to a grinding standstill. Some of them overturned, especially toward the front of the train, but other cars stayed upright, albeit leaning at crazy angles.

The doors of the first boxcar in line had been smashed open by the wreck. The riders swept in out of the darkness toward it. They had a wagon with them now, the vehicle having been parked out of sight of the tracks earlier. Several men leaped off their horses and ran toward the boxcar. A shotgun boomed from inside the wreckage. Someone was alive in there.

But not for long. The outlaws had their guns already drawn, and they poured lead into the shattered car for almost a minute. Then they ran forward again and climbed into the wreckage. They emerged a moment later, each man carrying a good-sized wooden crate. They took the crates to the wagon and loaded them into the back, then returned for more.

Meanwhile, the ones who had stayed on horseback stood guard.

Every time someone tried to poke a head out of one of the passenger cars, a flurry of gunshots drove them back. "Hurry it up!" one of the riders shouted at the men unloading the boxcar.

It didn't take long to empty the car of its cargo. The man who had been driving the wagon leaped back onto the seat and grabbed up the reins, whipping the team of sturdy mules into a run. He turned the wagon around and headed it to the north. Clouds of dust billowed up from its wheels and the hooves of the team and blurred the pinpoints of light that marked the stars in the night sky.

The rest of the gang followed at a gallop. They left behind a wrecked train, four dead men, several more who were badly injured, and a couple of dozen passengers who were shaken up considerably.

The rider who had so carefully positioned the glass bottle on the tracks was in the middle of the group, thinking bleak thoughts. Killing sure was easier the more you did of it.

Longarm stood there in the deserted house for several long minutes, trying to decide whether or not he was a damned fool. That seemed pretty likely to him, but the reason for drawing that conclusion was still open to debate.

He took the lantern and went outside, using its glow to study the ground all the way around the house. He found horse tracks behind the dwelling. Several riders had come here and stopped for a few minutes. Longarm could tell that by the droppings. There were a couple of cigarette butts on the ground too, indicating that the riders had had time to smoke quirlies. Then the riders had moved around the side of the house and out onto the main street, where the tracks disappeared in the welter of other hoofprints. It was impossible to distinguish one set of tracks from any other.

Longarm went back in Maggie's house and searched it again, from one end to the other. Nothing seemed to be missing. She might have just stepped out for a moment, from the way things looked.

Longarm knew that wasn't what had happened, though he couldn't have said what actually *had* occurred here tonight. Had those riders taken Maggie with them . . . or had she gone with them willingly? Was she a prisoner, or one of them? Had she even been in the house when they arrived, or had she left earlier?

He had no proof that the group of men who had visited Maggie's house tonight were Simon Dugan and his gang of bank robbers. But Longarm's instincts told him that was the most likely explanation. Who else would have had a reason to sneak up to Maggie's house in the dark the way these men had done?

But if he was right about the nocturnal visitors having been Dugan's bunch, what did they want with Maggie? Timothy Flynn was dead, killed in prison. Wasn't he?

Longarm stiffened at that thought. He had only Maggie's word for it that her husband was actually dead. Could she have been lying? Maybe she really believed Flynn was dead because that was what she'd been told. Maybe that was what she was supposed to believe.

With a puff of breath, Longarm blew out the lantern and replaced it in the kitchen where he'd found it. It wasn't going to do him any good to keep poking around Maggie's house. And with no trail he could follow, the only hope he had of finding her seemed to be the slim chance that Timothy Flynn was really still alive. That was something he could check on.

He went back out to his horse and swung up into the saddle. Wearily, he heeled the animal into motion. He had already ridden a long way today.

But he still had a ride in front of him, Longarm knew.

He retraced the route he had taken earlier from the flag stop, ignoring the growling from his belly as he rode. Sure, he was hungry, but it was more important that he get a handle on what was going on around here.

The little settlement that had grown up around the flag stop was ablaze with lights as Longarm approached it from the north. He frowned in puzzlement as he saw that seemingly every lamp and lantern in town had been lit. A train was stopped at the tiny depot, its engine huffing and wheezing. Folks scurried around like ants in a stepped-on mound.

Longarm pulled the bay to a halt in front of a hardware store. The store's front door was wide open, and several men came out carrying picks and shovels. Longarm lifted a hand and hailed them. "What's going on here, gents?"

All but one of the men ignored him and hurried on toward the depot, and the one who stopped did so grudgingly. He said, "Ain't you heard, mister?"

"Heard what?"

"There was a bad train wreck west of here. Locomotive derailed and took most of the rest of the cars with it. Kilt the engineer and the foreman. The conductor wasn't hurt too bad, though, so he was able to shinny up a telegraph pole and cut in on the line to get a message back here. The Western Union operator sent for a relief train, and we're loadin' up now to go see if we can lend a hand."

Longarm nodded his thanks, and the man trotted on down the street toward the tracks. Longarm sat and thought for a minute, then rode on to the depot himself. The building wasn't much bigger than an outhouse, just big enough for a ticket agent's window and a telegraph key. The two men who worked there as ticket agents for the railroad also doubled as telegraph operators, and that was where the telegraph office was located. One of the agents was standing on the postage-stamp platform in front of the depot, wearing an eyeshade even though it was night. He was not the man who had been on duty earlier in the day when Longarm was there.

Longarm tied the bay to a post and stepped up onto the platform. The train was still sitting there, fairly bulging with volunteers it had picked up on its run west from wherever it had started—Hays City, most likely. Longarm opened his mouth to speak to the agent, but before any words could come out, the train's shrill whistle sounded, drowning out everything else. Hard on the heels of the whistle came the clatter and squeal of drivers engaging and wheels beginning to turn on the rails. With a big puff of smoke from its stack, the train pulled out and rolled west.

The agent turned to Longarm. "You want something, mister? I'm kind of busy right now."

"Need to send a telegram," Longarm said.

The agent shook his head and began, "Come back in the morning—"

Longarm slipped a leather folder from his pocket and opened it so that the light from the lantern above the platform shone on the badge pinned to the inside. "Federal marshal," he said curtly.

"Oh. Well, in that case . . ." The agent shrugged. "Come on in, Marshal."

Longarm followed the man into the narrow, cramped confines of the station. The agent slipped behind the counter and sat down at the telegraph key. He tapped it a couple of times, then looked up at Longarm and asked, "You want to write out your message or just tell it to me?"

"I'll just tell it," Longarm said. "The message goes to Chief Marshal Billy Vail in Denver." The key started to click as the operator began sending. "Say to him: Need status of inmate Timothy Flynn Kansas State Penitentiary. Stop. Wire soonest. Stop. Sign it Long."

It took only a few seconds for the operator to complete the message. He glanced up at Longarm and asked, "You want to wait for a reply?"

Longarm didn't figure Vail would get the message until the next morning, and it would take a while for him to wire the authorities in Kansas and find out what had really happened to Timothy Flynn. So Longarm shook his head and said, "No, I'll come by about the middle of the day to-morrow—"

The telegraph key began to chatter.

The operator snatched up a stub of pencil and started scribbling words on a piece of paper as he listened intently to the series of dots and dashes coming over the wire. "This is for you, Marshal," he said without breaking his concentration.

Longarm's eyes widened in surprise. How could Billy Vail have gotten back in touch with him so fast? Vail must have been practically squatting on a telegraph key in Denver, Longarm thought.

The clicking stopped. The operator wrote a few more letters, then handed the message to Longarm through the opening of the ticket window. "Hope I got it all right," he said.

Quickly, Longarm scanned the message, then read it again a second time more slowly:

FORGET LITTLE ELM JOB **STOP** INVESTIGATE TRAIN
WRECK NEAR YOUR LOCATION **STOP** SEE CONDUCTOR
REGARDING SPECIAL SHIPMENT **STOP** TOP PRIORITY
STOP VAIL.

What the hell?

Orders were orders. Longarm wished he had gotten these a few minutes earlier, before that relief train pulled out. He said to the agent, "How far west of here is that crash?"

"Seven or eight miles."

That meant more riding. Longarm and the bay gelding were both getting worn out, but the night wasn't over. Longarm nodded his thanks to the agent, then turned and walked out of the little building.

It was easy to follow the railroad tracks, even at night. Longarm kept the bay at a steady, ground-eating trot. A little less than an hour later, he spotted lights up ahead. Lanterns were scattered out along the railroad right-of-way for what looked like a quarter of a mile, and in places, makeshift torches had been lit and stuck in the ground to give even more light.

As Longarm drew nearer, he was able to make out the shape of the relief train and beyond it the wreckage of the train that had derailed. The devastation stood out sharply in the harsh lantern light. Men were leading shaken passengers from the wrecked train and helping them onto the cars that had been brought out from the flag stop. Rough medical attention was being given to those who required it.

Longarm rode along the edges of the crowd and searched for the conductor of the derailed train. He finally spotted a stocky man in a blue suit, mostly bald with a fringe of white hair around his ears and bushy white eyebrows. The man had a smear of dried blood on his face from a bad cut on his forehead. He was waving his arms and shouting as he directed the relief operation.

Longarm dismounted and tied the bay to a stubby greasewood bush. He walked over to the man in the blue suit and asked, "You the conductor from that wrecked train?"

"That's right," the man snapped impatiently in a rather high-pitched voice. "What do you want?"

Longarm lowered his voice a little. "I'm U.S. Deputy Marshal Long. My orders are to talk to you about a special shipment on this train."

The conductor turned sharply toward him. "You know about it?"

"Only what I just told you," Longarm said.

The conductor grasped Longarm's sleeve. "Come on. Let's find some place we can talk in private." He seemed mighty anxious about something. "By the way, my name's Ollie Thurston."

Longarm allowed Thurston to tug him toward the far side of the tracks, opposite the side where the train had derailed. As they walked, their boots crunching on the cinders of the roadbed, they passed a section of track that was torn up badly. There was a crater in the roadbed, and one of the rails was broken and twisted. The other rail bulged out grotesquely but had not come apart.

"What in Hades happened here?" Longarm asked.

"That's what caused us to derail," Thurston said. "Some son of a bitch blew the tracks right out from under us."

Chapter 11

Longarm stared at the hole in the roadbed and the twisted rails for a long moment. It must have taken an awfully powerful explosive to cause such destruction, he thought. Something like nitroglycerine.

"Marshal?" Ollie Thurston said.

Longarm nodded and swung around toward the conductor again. They walked about twenty feet beyond the rails. With all the hubbub that was going on around the wrecked train, no one else would be able to overhear their conversation.

"Now, why don't you tell me what this is all about," Longarm suggested.

Thurston took a handkerchief from the pocket of his blue coat and mopped sweat from his forehead. The handkerchief came away stained with blood from the cut. "Money," Thurston said. "Lots of it."

"More than you usually carry on a run like this?"

"There was a whole boxcar full of paper money. Old bills that have been pulled out of circulation. They were being sent back to the Mint in Denver to be burned."

Longarm frowned. He knew that from time to time old bills were destroyed, but until they were, they were still legal tender. A boxcar full of currency, even though most of the bills were probably only rumpled old fives and tens, would still add up to one hell of a lot of money.

"I didn't know the Mint was in the habit of shipping old money on regular trains," Longarm said.

"This was special, one of the biggest shipments that's ever been put together," Thurston said. "The officials at the Mint wanted it kept secret. That's why it was crated up like regular freight and loaded onto a boxcar in Kansas City. Nothing fancy about it."

"Hiding it in plain sight, I reckon you could say."

Thurston nodded. "That's right. There were two guards traveling in the boxcar. The thinking was that any more than that might draw unwanted attention. The money was supposed to get to Denver without anybody even being aware of it."

That was a typical plan, Longarm thought, and might have even worked, but it was vulnerable in one particular area. At least a handful of people had to know about the old money that was on its way to a fiery end.

"Who on the train knew about it?" he asked.

"Just me and Carney Wilkes, the engineer," Thurston replied.

"And where's Wilkes now?" Longarm asked, although he figured he already knew the answer.

Thurston gestured toward the mangled wreckage of the locomotive. "Dead," he said grimly. "He and the fireman, Ben Granger, were killed almost instantly, I reckon." The conductor bristled a little. "Carney wouldn't have told anybody about the money, if that's what you're thinking, and I know that I damned sure didn't."

"What about the guards in the boxcar?"

"Both dead. From what I've been able to piece together from talking to the passengers, one of the guards survived the wreck, but when he tried to protect the money from the men who rode in, they gunned him."

This was the first Longarm had heard of riders attacking the train, but he wasn't surprised. Nobody would go to the trouble of blowing the train off the tracks unless they intended to loot the boxcar where the old currency was being carried.

Thurston went to fill him in on how the raiders had emptied the boxcar of its valuable freight. "They rode off to the north with the back of that wagon full of crates," he concluded.

"Did they get all the money?"

Thurston shook his head. "Some of the crates busted open in the crash and scattered currency all over the place. But they took all the crates that were still intact, and I'd be willing to wager they stuffed their pockets full of loose bills too."

Longarm agreed that was likely. "How many of them were there? Did anybody get a good look?"

"No, not really. It was dark, and the passengers were all scared shitless from the wreck. There must have been at least half a dozen, maybe more."

Longarm nodded. "And they headed north?"

"That's right." Thurston leaned forward, blinking birdlike. "Are you going after them, Marshal?"

"I reckon that's my job," Longarm said. "Won't be able to pick up the trail until dawn, though. Besides, my horse is done in, and I am too. Thought I'd go back to town and get a little rest and something to eat, pick up a fresh horse in the morning."

"I reckon that'd be best, all right. I sure hope you catch up to those bastards, Marshal. Carney Wilkes was a friend of mine, and I don't like anybody messing with my train."

"I'll get 'em," Longarm pledged. "One way or the other."

On his way back to the settlement, Longarm thought about the derailment and the robbery of the train. Someone must have known about the shipment of old money. The outlaws wouldn't have gone to the trouble of blowing up the tracks unless they knew for sure there would be a good payoff. Longarm had believed Thurston when the conductor said he hadn't told anyone about the crates full of currency, and although Longarm couldn't question the engineer, Carney Wilkes, he figured it was likely Wilkes hadn't said anything either. Wilkes certainly wouldn't have been part of any plot to derail the train, knowing that he would almost surely be killed in the wreck. He could have let something slip inadvertently, however.

Longarm considered it more likely that someone at the Denver Mint had fed the information to the gang. An inside man at the Mint could have set up the robbery without having to risk his own hide.

Then there was the question of who the actual robbers were, and Longarm already had a possible answer for that. Billy Vail had ordered him to drop the investigation into the explosions and bank robbery in Little Elm, but the way Longarm saw it, there was a good chance that raid was connected to what had happened tonight. The mysterious Simon Dugan had to be behind both crimes. The looting of the boxcar definitely fell under federal jurisdiction, so Longarm didn't have to worry about that anymore.

He was mighty worried, though, about who had handled the explosives in both cases.

When he reached the settlement, Longarm returned the bay to the livery stable where he had rented it a couple of days earlier. "I'll be back in the morning to rent another mount," he told the elderly hostler. Then he headed for the only hotel in town, where he rented a room, climbed the stairs wearily, and sprawled out on the narrow bed fully dressed except for his hat, boots, and gunbelt.

The sky was still dark when he woke up, but it was turning gray in the east. He splashed some water on his face, but didn't take the time to shave. The hotel had a dining room attached to it, so he was able to get some breakfast there. The bacon was overcooked and the flapjacks doughy in the middle, but the coffee was black and strong and bracing. When he was finished, he walked down the street to the livery stable, lighting a cheroot as he went.

The sun was not yet up, but the eastern sky was orange now instead of gray.

The old man led out a brown mare. Longarm's McClellan saddle was already cinched tight on the horse. "Best mount I got right now," the hostler told Longarm. "You wore that poor bay to a frazzle."

"Sorry," Longarm said. "I'm still a mite weary myself."

"Heard about the train wreck?" the hostler asked avidly. He was probably eager to exchange gossip.

Longarm wasn't in the mood. He just nodded and said, "Yep." He handed a twenty-dollar gold piece to the old man. "Don't know when I'll be back, so don't worry if I'm gone for a few days."

The hostler used the few teeth he had left in his mouth to bite down on the coin, then nodded in satisfaction. "Whatever you say, mister."

The general store on the other side of the street was already open. Longarm stopped there and picked up a few supplies, then rode out, headed west along the railroad tracks.

Some of the other early risers in the hotel dining room had been talking about the wreck, and Longarm had heard that the relief train had come back in during the night. A repair train was supposedly on the way from Hays City, but it would be later in the day before it reached the scene of the derailment and the workers began putting the damage right. Until then, no westbound trains could get through to Denver.

Longarm followed the tracks to the site of the catastrophe. The wreckage of the train was still scattered alongside the roadbed. Several armed railroad workers had been left behind to stand guard, and one of them challenged Longarm as he rode up.

"Federal marshal," he said as he opened the folder containing his badge and bona fides. "I'm going to try to pick up the trail of the gang that did this."

"Hope you catch the bastards, Marshal," the railroad man

97

said. "You ought to have a posse with you, though."

Longarm hadn't even considered that. He was a loner by nature, though he could work efficiently enough with other men when he needed to. Besides, the way Dugan's gang had so easily given the slip to all the posses that had chased them in the past, he figured one man would stand just as good a chance of finding them, maybe even a better chance.

He just waved farewell to the guards and sent the mare trotting northward. It took him only a few minutes to run across the narrow tracks left by the wheels of the wagon. The tracks were fairly deep, indicative of the load the vehicle was carrying. Crates full of paper money must be heavy, Longarm thought.

It was hard to tell exactly how many horses had accompanied the wagon. At least half a dozen, Longarm judged. That was what Ollie Thurston had pegged as the minimum number of robbers.

The tracks weren't difficult to follow. They ran almost as straight as an arrow toward the hills Longarm had explored the day before. Somewhere up there was the outlaws' hideout, Longarm was sure of it. When he found the place, would he find Maggie Flynn as well? Or her supposedly dead husband, or both?

Only one way to find out, he told himself.

He reached the hills at mid-morning, and after that, following the trail became harder. It disappeared on rocky stretches of ground, but he was always able to pick it up again on the far side. The robbers didn't appear to be going to any trouble to hide their tracks. By the time the sun was directly overhead at midday, Longarm was deep in the hills. He stopped to sleeve sweat off his face, let the mare rest, and gnaw on a piece of the jerky he had bought at the general store early that morning. Sitting in the shade of a bush while the horse cropped on some tufts of bunch grass, Longarm washed down the rawhide-tough meat with a swig of water from his canteen. He was still tired, and his eyes

98

felt gritty from not enough sleep the night before. Without even being aware of it, he began to doze.

His head jerked up abruptly. He had no idea how much time had passed since he nodded off, nor of what had woken him up. But as he looked around and listened intently, he heard a faint clinking sound: a horseshoe against rock.

Longarm came up off the ground in one smooth motion. A fast step took him to the side of the mare. He grabbed her reins and led her toward a brush-choked gully. That was the closest hiding place.

From the sound of the hoofbeats that were now audible, the rider was approaching from around the shoulder of a hillside, but whoever it was had not yet come into sight. The air was still, so Longarm's mount and the other horse had not caught each other's scent. Longarm still had a chance to get into cover before the stranger saw him.

The mare didn't much want to go into the gully, and Longarm didn't really blame her. The brush caught and clawed at them before springing back into its original position. Holding tightly to the reins, Longarm worked his way into the thicket and hauled the horse with him. Once he was convinced that they couldn't be spotted easily, he stopped and held his left hand over the mare's nose to keep her quiet.

It was unlikely that anyone who knew him would cross his path out here in these isolated hills. If the rider was one of the outlaw gang, however, he might be a little trigger-happy, eager to dispose of anyone who could stumble across the hideout.

There was another possibility: The rider could be Maggie Flynn. In that case, Longarm wanted to keep an eye on the young woman and see what she was up to before revealing his presence.

Carefully, he parted some of the brush so that he could peer out of his hiding place. His eyes narrowed as he studied the limited field of view. He could still hear the horse, but he couldn't see the rider.

There! A big, light-colored stallion crossed in front of the gully. It was prancing along somewhat nervously, and Longarm knew it had probably smelled the mare.

The man riding the stallion leaned forward and patted its shoulder. "What's the matter, boy?" he asked in a deep, resonant voice.

Longarm had never seen the man before. He appeared to be medium-sized, although that was hard to tell when a man was on horseback, and wore black whipcord pants, a dusty gray shirt, and a broad-brimmed black hat with its crown creased in a Montana pinch. He sported two guns in a tied-down gunfighter's rig, silver-plated Colts with ivory-inlaid grips. Fancy guns, the sort a dude from back East might carry. They were the only things fancy about the man, however. His features under the wide brim of the hat were tanned to the color of old saddle leather, and his eyes were keen. He sat a saddle as if he had been born to it. Longarm knew a dangerous man when he saw one, and he was looking at just such an hombre right now. He wondered if the man was Simon Dugan.

The stranger clearly sensed that something was wrong, but as he looked around, he couldn't see anything out of the ordinary. He rode on, out of Longarm's view. Longarm kept his hand on the mare's nose until the hoofbeats had faded away completely, and then waited a few more minutes for good measure before he pushed his way back out of the thicket.

His nerves were stretched taut. The stranger had been suspicious, and he had looked wily enough so that Longarm wouldn't have put it past him to slip out of the saddle and send the stallion on to draw out whoever had been watching. Longarm was ready for trouble.

None came, however. A quick check around the area told him that the stranger had indeed moved on. It occurred to Longarm that the stranger might be trailing the outlaw

100

gang, just as he himself was. That led to all sorts of interesting questions.

The only way to answer them was to push on. Longarm was even more careful now.

The hills became more rugged. Longarm hadn't penetrated this deeply into them on his previous visit. There was nothing in the whole state of Kansas that could even remotely be called a mountain by anybody except a flatlander, but some of the rocky promontories that stuck up from the ground around there were honest-to-goodness hills. Longarm spotted one particularly tall peak in the distance to the northwest and recognized it as Mount Sunflower. The Colorado border wasn't too many miles to the west, he figured. He was probably forty miles or more as the crow flies from Little Elm.

His mouth tightened into a grim line under the sweeping longhorn mustache as he realized the tracks of the gang he had been following had disappeared again. Nor was there any sign of the man he had seen earlier. Fighting feelings of disgust and frustration, Longarm pushed on, holding the mare to a walk so that it wouldn't make too much noise.

He drew rein at the top of a rise and studied the scene spread out before him. The ground sloped away into a vast bowl that ended abruptly about five hundred yards away where a gray cliff thrust up sheerly. Longarm figured the cliff was at least a hundred feet tall. It ran east and west as far as the eye could see. A man might be able to ride around it, but that was liable to take half a day or more. A line of trees grew along the base of the cliff, and Longarm wondered if there was a stream there. The rest of the huge bowl was largely barren.

A flicker of motion caught Longarm's attention. He leaned forward in the saddle and narrowed his eyes, squinting against the afternoon light. He studied the cliff intently, waiting for whatever he had seen before to make another appearance.

There it was again! Longarm frowned and muttered, "What the hell?"

He wished he had a telescope or a pair of field glasses. At this distance, he couldn't be sure if he was really seeing what he thought he was seeing.

But as far as he could tell, the stranger he had seen earlier was over there on the other side of the bowl, climbing the sheer face of that cliff like a damned fly.

Chapter 12

Obviously, the cliff face wasn't as smooth as it appeared to be from a distance. Otherwise, the man wouldn't be able to climb it like that. He moved slowly, making certain of each foothold and handhold before he trusted his weight to it. His route angled back and forth as he searched out the easiest and safest way to the top.

Longarm couldn't see what was beyond the cliff, but it had to be something pretty interesting to make a man risk that climb. He jogged the mare into a walk. The horse began picking its way across the bowl. Longarm wasn't worried about the man on the cliff spotting him; that gent had other things on his mind right now, such as not making a misstep and falling to his death.

As Longarm rode toward the cliff, he kept an eye on the man climbing it. The man was almost at the top by the time Longarm reached the trees along the base of the cliff. He eased the horse into the cottonwoods and reined in, seeing that the trees did indeed line the bank of a small stream. On the opposite side of the creek was the cliff itself. The leafy branches would shield him from being spotted from above, but they also prevented him from keeping track of the climber's progress. Longarm swung down from the saddle and ground-hitched the mare, then went to the edge of the trees and tilted his head back to peer upward.

He was just in time to see the stranger disappear over the top of the cliff.

Longarm's horse whinnied. He recognized the sound: The mare had caught the scent of the stranger's mount. Longarm searched quickly through the trees, and found the big stallion tied to one of the cottonwoods about fifty yards away from the spot where he'd left the mare. The stallion tossed its head menacingly as Longarm approached.

"Hold on there, old son," Longarm said in a soothing voice. "I don't mean any harm. I just want to take a look in those saddlebags and see if I can figure out who your owner is."

The stallion backed away as far as the tied reins would allow it, and it bared its teeth at Longarm as he came closer. Longarm kept talking, though, and after a few minutes the stallion began to relax. The animal allowed Longarm to move alongside it and even to lightly stroke its shoulder. The stallion trembled a little under Longarm's touch, but he knew it wasn't afraid of him. It was just trying to decide whether or not to bite his fingers off.

"That's it, old son," Longarm murmured. "Wish I had an apple with me. We'd share it, one bite at a time. Better an apple than my hand, eh?"

The stranger's saddle was smooth black leather with a horn that flared out wide at the top, the sort of rig a Texas cowboy might use. A sheathed Winchester was strapped to the opposite side of the saddle from where Longarm stood. The rifle's stock was polished walnut with a black rubber butt and elaborate scrollwork further up toward the grip. An expensive weapon, and obviously well cared for.

Longarm reached for the flap of the saddlebag on his side and lifted it. He slipped his hand inside and found only a box of .44 shells and some hard, cloth-wrapped biscuits. The bag on the other side contained a pair of socks, a Barlow knife, and a spare gray shirt like the one the man was wearing. The shirt seemed to be wrapped around something, however, so Longarm removed it from the saddlebag and unwrapped it.

Inside the shirt was a small bundle of envelopes, bound together with a string. Evidently they were letters from a woman, because each of the envelopes had an address written on it in a feminine hand. The ink was faded, as if the envelopes had been addressed years ago. The addresses themselves changed with almost every envelope, Longarm saw as he flipped through them without untying the string. They ranged from Texas to Montana, from Missouri to California, and almost every place in between.

But the name on the envelopes never varied. Every one of them was addressed to Mr. Dan Boyd.

"Well, now, Mr. Boyd," Longarm said as he glanced up toward the top of the cliff, "I know who you are now, even if I don't know what you're doing out here."

He wrapped up the letters in the shirt and replaced them in the saddlebag, pondering what he had learned. The man he had followed here wasn't Simon Dugan after all—unless either Dugan or Boyd was an alias and the other was the man's real name.

Curiosity made Longarm wade across the shallow creek to the base of the cliff. He laid a hand on its rocky face and leaned back slightly to peer up. As he had supposed, the cliff wasn't nearly as sheer as it had appeared from a distance. There were plenty of handholds and footholds in the form of narrow ledges that had been carved into it. For a moment Longarm thought the ledges were man-made, but closer examination told him they were natural, probably a result of whatever ancient geologic upheaval that had thrust up the cliff and dropped the adjacent ground into the bowl.

Longarm knew that some gents climbed mountains and rocks and cliffs for the pure pleasure they got out of it, and he'd never thought that made a lick of sense. The only good reason to climb something was a need to get to the top.

In this case, he needed to find out what was beyond the cliff and what it had to do with a mysterious stranger named

Dan Boyd. And the only way to do that was to follow in Boyd's footsteps.

Longarm took a deep breath, reached up for a handhold, and started hauling himself up the cliff.

The first part of the climb was fairly easy, but the angle grew steeper the farther up he went. When he got high enough so that the trees no longer shaded him, the sun beat against him hotly. Beads of sweat popped out on his forehead and dripped into his eyes so that he had to blink them away. His shirt grew damp. Muscles that were unaccustomed to this particular form of exertion began to ache.

He paused occasionally to rest, but after the first glance down during one of those breaks, he didn't try that again. He had never been particularly scared of heights, but there was no point in tempting fate. It was just human nature for a fella to get a little dizzy whenever he looked down and saw nothing underneath him but a lot of empty air.

Longarm was careful not to dislodge any rocks that would clatter down the slope beneath him. If Boyd was still close by the top of the cliff, such noises would warn him that someone else was on the way up. Just about the last thing Longarm wanted in this situation was to have somebody above him trying to stop him.

It seemed as if two or three hours had passed since he started climbing the cliff, but he knew it was more like half an hour as he approached the summit at last. It was another in a long series of nerve-wracking moments as he prepared to pull himself up and over the brink. He paused and listened intently for several minutes, trying to determine by sound if anyone was close by up there, but he didn't hear a thing except some distant birds. Finally, he reached up to the last handhold and raised himself so that he could see over the edge.

The ground beyond the cliff was level, covered with sparse grass, and dotted in places with clumps of scrubby trees. Longarm watched for a couple of minutes and saw nothing moving.

He pulled himself over the top of the cliff and sprawled out on the ground for a moment. His legs were shaky, and he was afraid if he tried to stand up right now, they would buckle under him like those of a newborn colt. Strength flowed back into his body along with the deep breaths he dragged into his lungs, and after a few minutes, he felt steady enough to roll over and push himself to his feet.

Once he was upright, he could see that the ground dropped away again about a hundred yards north of the cliff. Whether it was sheer over there or a more gentle slope, he didn't know, but he intended to find out. He started in that direction, keeping a close eye out for any warning of trouble.

As Longarm approached the far edge, he crouched, not wanting to skyline himself to anyone watching from below. After a few more yards, he went to hands and knees and crawled forward, finally bellying down so that he was in position to peer over the edge without exposing himself. He saw right away that there wasn't a cliff on this side; instead, the terrain fell away in a series of steep but manageable benches. At the bottom of them was a narrow valley bounded on the other three sides by more cliffs. A stream meandered through the center of the valley, and Longarm wondered if it connected somehow with the creek that flowed at the base of the cliff he had climbed. That seemed likely.

What interested him more than the geography was the presence of a couple of small log cabins below him in the valley. They had been built next to the creek, and beyond them was a pole corral where about a dozen horses were penned up. Longarm didn't see any people moving around, but he was sure somebody was in one of the cabins: Smoke came from the stone chimney on one end of the structure.

Longarm knew he was looking at the hideout of the gang that had derailed the train and stolen the old money. Chances were, they were also the bunch that had blown up half of Little Elm and robbed the bank there. He understood now why the posses that had trailed them in the past had never been able to find them. No one would ever stumble over this hidden fold in the landscape unless it was by pure accident.

There had to be another way in and out of the valley. The gang's horses had never climbed that cliff. Longarm suspected there might be an underground passage where that stream ran on its way to join the one outside. If that was the case, the outer opening was probably well concealed, so that anyone who didn't know it was there would never find it.

Where was Dan Boyd? Longarm hadn't seen him since Boyd had reached the top of the cliff. Was he already down there in one of those cabins? Meeting, maybe, with Simon Dugan?

Suddenly, Longarm saw a flicker of movement down below. Dan Boyd darted out of a clump of brush on one of the benches and slid down the slope to the next one, then immediately hunkered down behind some rocks. Longarm's mouth quirked in a humorless grin. Boyd was sneaking up on the outlaws, just as Longarm was sneaking up on Boyd. There sure was a lot of skulking going on around here this afternoon.

Even more than he had thought, he realized abruptly a moment later when a figure silently glided out from behind some trees and started closing in on Boyd's back. The newcomer was tall and dressed in range clothes, a battered black hat on his head and several days' worth of beard stubble on his face. He was carrying a rifle, and from the looks of things, he was about to jump Boyd, maybe even bushwhack him and shoot him in the back.

Longarm wondered what the hell he was supposed to do now.

Before he could ponder the question for very long, things started to happen. Boyd must have heard the fellow sneaking up behind him, because he twisted around suddenly just as the man lunged at him, rifle upraised to strike down with the butt. Neatly, Boyd avoided the blow and thrust his foot between the ankles of the other man, tripping him. The man was already startled by Boyd's whirlwind reaction, and he had no chance to stay on his feet. He sprawled on the ground and Boyd kicked the rifle out of his hands.

Longarm's brain moved just as rapidly as the flurry of action he was watching. The scruffy-looking gent had to be a sentry posted by the outlaws. That might mean Boyd's purposes ran contrary to those of Dugan's gang. Which could make him a potential ally for Longarm . . .

Or something even better: a way in.

One of the ivory-handled Colts leaped into Boyd's hand. He backed off a couple of steps, covering the fallen guard, and said in a voice that carried to Longarm, "Don't move, fella. I'd hate to have to kill you."

The range was a little farther than Longarm liked, but he had no choice. He drew his own revolver as he straightened from his crouch, and he leveled it at Boyd as he called, "Drop it!"

Boyd tensed, and Longarm knew he was on the verge of whipping around to meet this new threat. Longarm fired, deliberately aiming wide so that the bullet kicked up dirt a dozen feet to Boyd's right. The shot would bring the rest of the gang on the run, but right now that was exactly what Longarm wanted.

"I said drop it, mister!" he shouted to Boyd. "The next one goes right between your shoulder blades."

That would be an awfully tricky shot at this range, even for Longarm, but Boyd didn't have to know that. A couple of heartbeats went by, and then Boyd gave a little shrug and leaned over to place the ivory-handled Colt on the ground.

Longarm went down the hill quickly, covering Boyd all the way. While he was doing that, the guard scrambled to his feet and ran to retrieve the rifle Boyd had kicked away from him. He snatched it off the ground and started to turn around, his face contorting into a rage-filled snarl as he did so. By that time, Longarm was sliding down onto the same bench and was about twenty feet away. He saw the hate in the sentry's eyes and knew the man was liable to put a slug in Boyd just out of sheer meanness and injured pride. Longarm switched his aim to the guard and snapped, "Hold it! No need for any killing."

"Much obliged," Boyd said dryly. He wore a half-smile on his weathered face. If he was overly disconcerted by this turn of events, he didn't show it.

"Who the hell are you?" the guard demanded. He didn't lower the rifle, but held it ready to use on either Longarm or Boyd, however things developed.

"A friend," Longarm said. "I came here looking for Simon Dugan and Maggie Flynn."

It was a long shot and he knew it, but he had played in enough high-stakes poker games to recognize the time to follow a hunch and run a bluff. The guard's eyes widened in surprise. He said, "How'd you know about Maggie?"

"Never mind that." From the corner of his eye, Longarm caught a flash of movement on the slope below. "If I ain't mistaken, here comes Dugan now."

Sure enough, five hombres came boiling out of a stand of trees and ran toward the little group consisting of Longarm, Boyd, and the sentry. The newcomers were all carrying guns. They stopped, and the man in the lead called, "What the hell's going on up there, Luke?"

Something about the voice was tantalizingly familiar to Longarm, but he couldn't place it right away. He kept a tight rein on his emotions, not wanting his surprise to show on his face. He hadn't expected to recognize anyone except maybe Maggie Flynn when he finally caught up to the gang.

The sentry—obviously named Luke—turned his head a little, but still didn't take his eyes off Longarm and Boyd. He called down, "Got a couple of strangers up here, Simon. One of 'em acts like he's a friend of yours."

Simon Dugan came closer and raised his head so that

110

Longarm got a look at his face under the broad brim of a high-crowned hat. He grinned and said, "Not a friend, but definitely an acquaintance, I reckon."

This time Longarm couldn't keep from staring.

Simon Dugan was Carl Thorne, owner of the Thorne House hotel in Little Elm.

Chapter 13

"Why, howdy there, Mr. Polk," Dugan—Thorne—whatever the hell his name was!—called up to Longarm. "I didn't expect to run into you way out here in the middle of nowhere. You must not have stayed in your room in the hotel last night. Did you move out? Hope you weren't unhappy with the service."

Surprised or not by this revelation of Simon Dugan's true identity, Longarm knew there was nothing he could do now except continue brazening it out. He said roughly, "Don't play games, Dugan. I'm here on business, just like you."

"Business? What sort of business would that be, Mr. Polk?" Dugan asked. "You told me you were a writer."

Longarm allowed a ghost of a smile to play across his face for a second. "Anybody ever told you how much those fellas get paid? There's more money in sidelines—like bank robbery."

"Sort of like running a hotel," Dugan said with a chuckle. "Are you saying you came out here to join us, Mr. Polk?"

Longarm glanced at the sentry. "If all of your boys fall down on the job like this, it seems like you could use some good help."

"Wait just a damned minute—" the guard began hotly, but Dugan stopped him with a raised hand.

"Hold on, Luke. Mr. Polk's just expressing an opinion, after all. A fella's got a right to do that." Dugan's gaze swung toward Boyd and grew colder. "And what about you, mister? What are you doing here?"

Boyd was still standing there, not looking overly concerned. He was an icy-nerved hombre, Longarm had to give him that much. "My name is Baxter," Boyd lied. "Maybe you've heard of me."

"Can't say as I—" Dugan paused abruptly and frowned. "Wasn't it somebody named Baxter who shot up a whole posse of deputy marshals down in the Nations a while back?"

Boyd shrugged nonchalantly. "Was it?"

One of the other men spoke up, saying, "Seems to me there was a hired gun called Baxter who fought on McSween's side in the Lincoln County War."

"Do tell," Boyd said coolly.

Dugan frowned suspiciously at him. "Are you claiming to be the same man?"

"All I'm saying," Boyd said, "is that I wanted to take a look at what was in here, and then your man jumped me."

"How'd you know the valley was back here behind the cliff?" Dugan asked.

"Stumbled on the tunnel down below where the stream runs. I knew it had to lead somewhere."

That confirmed one of Longarm's guesses anyway. Assuming that Boyd wasn't lying about it, he reminded himself, and despite the man's other falsehoods, Longarm couldn't see any reason for him not to tell the truth about that part of it.

"Why didn't you go through the tunnel, if you were so blasted curious?"

"I figured you'd have a guard or two posted there, so I decided to climb the cliff instead. When it wasn't as hard as it looks, I decided you'd have a guard up here too, but I knew I'd rather deal with him out in the open, rather than closed up in some hole in the ground."

113

From the sound of that, Boyd didn't care much for tunnels, Longarm thought. Must not have ever been around many mine shafts.

Slowly, Dugan shook his head. "Mister, you're a damned puzzle. I think I know why Polk came out here. He's been nosing around the area for a couple of days. You just dropped out of a clear blue sky."

"Not really," Boyd said. He glanced at Longarm. "I'm looking for the same thing as Mr. Polk: the gang that held up the bank in Little Elm last week and derailed a train last night."

So, Longarm thought, Boyd knew almost as much about the gang as he did. Boyd had to be a lawman of some sort, and Longarm felt a momentary twinge of guilt about exposing him to danger in order to try to win Dugan's confidence. But Boyd had the air of someone who'd been to see the elephant more than once; he had to know how much danger went with the badge when he pinned it on.

"Let me see if I've got this straight," Dugan said. "We've got two strangers poking their noses into our hidey-hole, one of them a writer and the other one a gunslinger. And both of you act like you want to join up with us."

Longarm looked at Boyd, and Boyd returned the look with a cool, unworried stare. "I reckon that's about the size of it," Longarm said.

"Hell with it," Dugan said sharply. "I don't trust either of you, and the best thing to do is kill you both."

His gun started to come up, and Longarm tensed, preparing to sell his life as dearly as possible. He hoped Boyd could use that left-hand gun and take a couple of the gang with him too.

"Wait!" a woman's voice called urgently.

Maggie Flynn came running out of the trees. Longarm looked at her and saw that she was dressed like a man, with denim trousers, high-topped boots, a jacket over a man's shirt, and a floppy-brimmed hat with her thick blond hair tucked up into it. She had a red checkered bandanna tied around her neck and a cartridge belt strapped around her hips. A walnut-butted Colt Navy .36 rode in the tied-down holster.

When he saw her, Longarm's heart sank a little. Even after Luke's reaction when he mentioned Maggie's name, Longarm had been hoping against hope that somehow he was wrong about her. He would have preferred that Timothy Flynn was still alive and setting off explosions for Dugan's gang. It might have been better even if Maggie had been a prisoner of the gang, because then Longarm could have worked on setting her free.

Clearly, however, she was here of her own free will.

And she must have learned a lot about nitroglycerine from her late husband, because Longarm would have been willing to bet that Maggie Flynn was handling the stuff now for Dugan.

The bandit leader turned his head without lowering his gun. "Blast it, Maggie," he said over his shoulder, "I told you to stay down in the cabin."

"Simon, you can't shoot that man," she protested as she hurried up to the group of men. "He's my friend Custis."

"Custis, huh," Dugan repeated. He glanced narrow-eyed at Longarm. "Told me his name was Polk. That's how he signed in at the hotel, as E. E Polk from Denver."

Quickly, Longarm searched the musty archives of his brain and dragged out the term he was looking for. "Ain't you ever heard of a pseudonym, Dugan? It means an alias for writers, sort of like Carl Thorne is an alias for an outlaw."

Dugan chuckled as some of his suspicion faded. "Yeah, it's a pretty respectable-sounding name, ain't it? I got a gal up in Nebraska to dye my hair and called myself Carl Thorne when I came back to Little Elm, and there wasn't a one of those dumb townies who recognized me."

"So you bought yourself a hotel with the money you got from the jobs you pulled with Tim Flynn and laid low for a while," Longarm guessed.

Dugan shot a glance at Maggie. "The two of you must've shared a whole heap of talk in bed," he said.

She blushed and said, "I told Custis all about Tim and how he fell in with you and your bunch, Simon."

"You didn't tell him everything, though, did you, pretty Maggie? You didn't tell him how *you've* turned desperado too, just like ol' Tim."

Boyd said, "This is mighty entertaining, but do you reckon we could put our hands down now? If you're not still planning on shooting us, that is."

"I wouldn't go around reminding folks of things like that," Longarm said.

Dugan looked back and forth between Longarm and Boyd for a moment and gritted his teeth in frustration. "All right," he said. "I guess there ain't no need to kill you two right away." He jerked his head in command. "Get their guns, boys. We'll go down and make ourselves comfortable; then we'll hash this out once and for all."

Longarm wished he could talk to Maggie, but there was no chance as he and Boyd were surrounded by the outlaws, disarmed, and marched down the hill toward the cabins in the valley. He was just glad they hadn't searched him, because his badge and his credentials were still in their leather folder, tucked away inside his jacket. If any of the owlhoots stumbled across those bona fides, likely they would be his death warrant.

Longarm glanced over at Dan Boyd as they walked—or at least at the man he *assumed* was Dan Boyd. This fella's name might really be Baxter, for all Longarm actually knew. He could have been in possession of those letters addressed to Boyd without actually being Boyd.

There was just too damned much he didn't know yet, Longarm thought. He had figured out that Maggie was working with the gang and had that theory confirmed, but as yet he didn't know why she had turned outlaw. He suspected her motive had something to do with the way the town of Little Elm had treated her after her husband was sent to prison. The natural resentment Maggie felt could have festered and turned into something even worse.

Then there was the matter of Simon Dugan really being Carl Thorne. Or was that vice versa? Dugan himself had pretty well explained that. He had gotten a thrill out of coming back in a new identity to a town that had despised him in the old identity. And what better hiding place could there be for a man who was still wanted? Once again, it was a case of hiding in plain sight.

Longarm glanced through the ring of outlaws around him and saw that Maggie was watching him. And Dugan was watching *her,* with a thoughtful expression on his face. Longarm couldn't help but wonder just what the relationship was between those two.

Longarm and Boyd were herded into the larger of the two cabins. Boyd sniffed the air and grinned. "Stew," he said. "Smells good."

"Maybe you can have a bowl of it later," Dugan said. "If you're not dead by then."

"I can always eat," Boyd said.

Dugan gestured toward a long, rough-hewn table. "Sit down, both of you," he ordered.

Longarm and Boyd settled down on a bench on the same side of the table. Dugan seated himself in a chair at the head of it and dropped his hat on the floor. He fished the makin's from his shirt pocket and started rolling a quirly.

"Tell me," he said, "just why I hadn't ought to go ahead and kill the both of you."

Maggie had taken off her hat and hung it on a nail just inside the door, allowing her hair to tumble loosely around her shoulders. She went to the black cast-iron stove and began stirring the contents of the pot that was simmering on it. She looked at Longarm, and for a second her hand dropped to the butt of the Colt Navy on her hip. She was behind Dugan and might be able to get the drop on him, although the other members of the gang would probably have something to say about that. Was she asking him if she ought to try it anyway? Longarm wondered. He looked at her and hoped she understood he wanted her to wait.

He had a few cards left to play before this hand was over.

"Well, I don't know about Mr. Polk," Boyd said in answer to Dugan's demand, "but I've never seen a bunch like this that couldn't use another good man. I've been drifting for a while, on my own, and when I heard about the jobs you've pulled lately, I thought that this would be a good group to throw in with."

"In other words, you want to horn in on what we've worked hard to get started," Dugan said.

Boyd's affable exterior began to show some signs of anger. "I pull my own weight," he snapped. "Ask anybody who's ever ridden with me."

"Where'll I find 'em?" Dugan asked coolly. "Behind bars . . . or in Boot Hill?"

Boyd shrugged. "Banditry is a profession with a lot of risks attached to it. You ought to know that, Dugan."

"How'd you know the same bunch hit Little Elm and derailed that train?"

"Because of the explosives involved. Nitroglycerine, wasn't it?"

Dugan leaned back in his chair. "You're a smart man, Baxter. Maybe too smart for your own good." He switched his gaze to Longarm. "What about you, Polk, or whatever your real name is? Are you smart too?"

"Smart enough to recognize a good thing when I see it," Longarm replied. He paused, then added, "Besides, this wouldn't be the first time I've worked with fellas like you."

"Is that so?"

"Who do you think tipped off the James boys every time the railroad dicks and the Pinkertons got too close to them?"

It was a bold lie, but one that Dugan probably couldn't dispute. Frank and Jesse James were lying low these days,

118

evidently retired from their notorious career, and there were even rumors that one or both of the James brothers were dead. Unless one of Dugan's gang happened to have ridden with the Jameses at one time or another, Longarm's falsehood was safe.

Evidently that was the case, because several of Dugan's men looked impressed and none of them called Longarm a liar. Even Dugan himself appeared to look at Longarm with a little more respect. He said, "Are you saying you know Frank and Jesse? Why would you help them?"

"A writer needs something to write about," Longarm said. "Outlaws make good stories."

"You ever write about Baxter here?"

Longarm glanced at Boyd. "No, but I reckon I've heard of him, all right, now that you mention it. Something about a shootout down in the Texas Panhandle, at a place called Tascosa. A gent named Baxter went into a saloon and killed four men in less than a minute."

That was a total fabrication, a web of fiction spun right out of his head. Maybe he ought to consider really becoming a writer when he retired, Longarm thought. Not that he was likely to live long enough to retire. But if he could help Boyd win entrance into the gang, maybe Boyd would lend a hand to him when the time came too.

Dugan looked at Boyd. "Is that true?"

"Lots of folks tell stories," Boyd drawled. "Most times, there's a kernel of truth in them."

Dugan sat up and placed both hands flat on the table. "Well, I don't know what to do," he said. "It's mighty suspicious, both of you showing up like this, uninvited, in a place a heap of lawmen would give their eyeteeth to find. On the other hand, you both make it sound like you've got good reasons for wanting to throw in with us." He looked around at his men. "What do you think we should do with them?"

"Safest thing would still be to kill 'em both," one of the outlaws said.

"No." That came from the stove, where Maggie Flynn had turned away from the pot of stew. "When Tim was riding with you, Simon, nobody ever got killed. Now you . . . you've gotten so bloodthirsty. . . ."

"You're the one who used the nitroglycerine, Maggie," Dugan said coldly.

Her face was pale, and Longarm could see the strain in her eyes. "I know. And I know I promised I'd help you in order to avenge Tim's death, but . . . but I never counted on so much killing. Why don't you let it end here, Simon?"

She was wasting her time with pleas like that, Longarm thought. No matter what Dugan might say, he was a ruthless, cold-blooded murderer, and that wasn't going to change. But he might try to placate Maggie by sparing Longarm and Boyd, at least for the time being. That was something to hope for anyway.

Dugan turned his attention back to the two visitors to the hideout. "I reckon we can give you two a chance," he said, and he held up a hand to forestall any protest from the other members of the gang. "You'll be unarmed while we're here in the hideout, and somebody will be keeping a pretty close eye on both of you. Try anything funny and you'll wind up dead in a hurry. I want to get to know you before I make up my mind for good."

"Say you decide to trust us," Boyd suggested. "What then?"

"Then you'll still have to prove yourselves. You'll have to go along with us on our next job." Dugan grinned. "After that, you'll be as guilty as any of the rest of us. If we swing, you do too."

"Fair enough," Longarm said.

"As fair as you're going to get," Dugan said, "and a hell of a lot better than a bullet in the head."

Longarm couldn't argue with that. He had accomplished the first step in his so-far nebulous plan. He had made it into the gang.

Now all he had to do was stay alive for a while and figure out what to do next.

Chapter 14

The stew tasted as good as it smelled. Longarm knew from experience that Maggie was a good cook. And he knew now that she could cook up a mess of nitroglycerine just as well as she could a pot of stew.

He was anxious to have a talk with her in private, but he didn't know when he would have that chance. Nor was he certain of what he would tell her when and if the opportunity presented itself. Despite her protest at the killing involved in the gang's jobs, she had participated in them, apparently of her own choosing. If Longarm revealed to her that he was really a lawman, she might turn on him and spill the truth to Dugan and the others. That would be a fast way to get dead.

He couldn't tell the truth to Boyd either, because the man's motives were still too murky to make out. Maybe Boyd, or Baxter, was really what he claimed to be: a gunman looking for a chance to clean up by joining an already successful gang of owlhoots.

When you came right down to it, Longarm thought, he couldn't really trust *anybody* in this isolated valley. That was all right, he decided. He had played many a lone hand before. Now it was time to play another one.

After they had eaten, Dugan sent a man out through the

tunnel to fetch the horses Longarm and Boyd had left tied in the trees at the base of the cliff. Longarm was anxious to get a look at that tunnel, but he supposed that would have to wait.

Darkness fell quickly in the valley, ringed as it was by higher ground. Dugan said to Longarm and Boyd, "You fellas will have to spread your soogans on the ground. All the bunks in the cabins are taken."

"Won't be the first time I've slept on the ground," Boyd said.

"Just don't get any ideas about sneaking out once it's good and dark," Dugan warned. "There'll be sentries on duty, and if anybody starts moving around, they won't ask questions. They'll just shoot."

He sauntered out onto the cabin's porch, motioning for Longarm and Boyd to follow him. As Dugan rolled a quirly, Longarm took out a cheroot and lit it. Boyd shook his head when Longarm offered him one of the little cigars. "I don't use 'em," Boyd said.

Dugan struck a lucifer and lit his cigarette. "I'll be heading back to Little Elm tonight," he said. "But I'll be back in a few days, and we'll see about getting ready for another job."

"Got to get back to the hotel?" Longarm asked.

Dugan grinned in the lantern light that spilled onto the porch through the open cabin door. "That's right. A successful business doesn't run itself, you know. Why, if I wanted to settle down and run a hotel the rest of my life, I could make a living at it. Never would get rich, though. And I'd rather put a bullet through my brain than be tied down in one place from now on." He glanced over his shoulder into the cabin. "Darlin' Maggie might've made me change my mind about that, but she wasn't having any of it. She didn't mind teaming up with me in order to get her revenge for what happened to Tim, but that's as far as it's gone."

Longarm felt a surge of relief at that statement. He had

never been the jealous sort, but it would have stuck in his craw to know that Maggie had been bedding down with a snake like Simon Dugan.

The outlaw chief took a couple of deep draws on the quirly, then flicked the butt away. "So long, Polk," he said. "You too, Baxter. Hope you boys ain't dead when I get back."

He stepped down from the porch and headed for the rope corral where the gang's horses were kept. Longarm watched him disappear into the darkness.

"There goes a smart man," Boyd said quietly. "But not a very likable one."

"You don't have to like a fella to cash in with him," Longarm said.

"That's true." Boyd paused, then continued. "Reckon I'll get my bedroll and turn in. Good night . . . Custis."

So Boyd remembered what Maggie had called him, Longarm thought. He wondered if Boyd recognized the name from somewhere.

The newcomers' gear had been piled in a lean-to built on the side of the main cabin. Boyd headed in that direction, moving with an easy, nonchalant gait. Longarm noticed one of the outlaws standing on the end of the porch, watching Boyd. The owlhoot had a Winchester cradled in the crook of his left arm. If Boyd did anything suspicious, Longarm figured the guard would cut him down without hesitation. Those had been Dugan's orders.

Longarm heard the faint sound of a horse's hooves fading in the distance. That would be Dugan riding out of the valley toward the tunnel. Longarm hoped the others could be counted on to do their leader's bidding. Dugan had said that he and Boyd were not to be harmed unless they tried something funny.

Longarm intended to be on his best behavior for the time being.

He decided that the best place to spread his bedroll would be under one of the trees alongside the creek. That was still well within sight of the cabin, so whoever had been detailed to guard him could easily keep an eye on him. When he was finished with the cheroot, he got his blankets and saddle from the lean-to and carried them over to the spot he had picked out. It took only a few moments to clear the ground of rocks and spread the bedroll. He took off his hat and gunbelt and stretched out, using the saddle as a pillow.

Even though he was very tired, Longarm found that sleep did not come easily. His mind kept going over everything that had happened since his arrival in Little Elm, and his thoughts kept returning to the derailment of the train and the theft of the old currency on its way to Denver to be destroyed.

Someone inside the Mint had to have fed Dugan the information about the shipment of money. Longarm had realized that right from the start. He had also realized that it wouldn't be enough to track down Dugan's gang. Billy Vail would want to know the identity of the inside man too. And the only way to find that out, Longarm had concluded, was from the inside.

So that was where he was now, he thought as he stared up at the stars floating in the clear Kansas sky.

A nearby step made his muscles tense. He lifted his head and saw the dark figure blotting out some of those twinkling pinpoints of light.

"Custis?" Maggie whispered.

Longarm lifted himself on an elbow and said quietly, "I'm here."

She dropped to her knees beside him and reached out to rest a hand on his shoulder. "Are you all right?"

"Fine as frog hair," he replied. "Why wouldn't I be?"

"I . . . I don't trust Simon. Not completely. I was worried that he might have told some of the others to sneak out here and kill you after he'd gone."

"Nobody has bothered me," Longarm assured her as he sat up. "I appreciate the concern, though."

"Why did you have to follow us? I was hoping that when

you came back to Little Elm and found me gone, you'd move on."

"I couldn't do that, Maggie," he said. "I was mighty worried about you. For all I knew, Dugan and his bunch had kidnapped you, maybe even hurt you."

She gave a short, humorless laugh. "Instead, you find out that I'm one of them, just as much an outlaw as anybody else in the gang."

"I reckon you had your reasons for whatever decisions you made," Longarm said.

"Damned right I did! The people in Little Elm made life miserable for me after Tim was arrested and sent to prison. I was left at the mercy of a heavy-handed lout like Brad Holcomb. Sooner or later, he would have gotten tired of taking no for an answer and would have hauled me out to his ranch whether I liked it or not! And not one person in that town would have lifted a finger to stop him, Custis. Not one."

Longarm believed her. He said, "I don't blame you for being mad at them. But you *did* blow up half the town and kill some folks."

"I didn't mean for anybody to be hurt! I didn't plan for Rory Pierce and Elsa to get caught in the explosions. The dynamite was set to go off in places that should have been deserted at that time of night."

"You used regular dynamite instead of nitroglycerine?" Longarm asked.

"A combination of the two," Maggie said. "I bundled a couple of sticks of dynamite with a jar of soup. That's what Tim always called it. That way I could set long fuses on the dynamite and when it exploded, it set off the nitroglycerine."

Longarm had to repress a shudder. No wonder the blasts had been so devastating. A thought suddenly occurred to him, and he said, "That first day I met you, when you were carrying that heavy box . . ." This time, he couldn't stop the cold chill that shivered up his backbone. "That wasn't a box full of nitroglycerine you almost dropped on the board-walk between us, was it?"

"Of course not."

Longarm heaved a sigh of relief.

"It was regular dynamite I was bringing from the hotel. Very unlikely that just dropping it could cause it to go off."

"But not impossible?"

"No," Maggie admitted. "Not impossible."

Longarm shook his head. "If I'd known what I was really carrying, I'd have been a mite more careful."

"There was no harm done," Maggie told him.

"What was Dugan doing with a box full of dynamite?"

"He has it shipped in from the East. The crates are al-ways marked as something else, usually hotel supplies or something like that. Then I take it back to my house and extract the nitroglycerine there."

"By boiling the dynamite?"

"Yes."

Longarm shook his head. Little Elm was lucky it hadn't been blown off the map before now. If the good citizens of the settlement had known what their innocent-looking schoolmarm was really cooking up in her kitchen . . .

"Why are you explaining all this to me now?" he asked her.

"You wanted the whole story," she said. "When you start to write about it, you'll need all the facts."

"Well, I'm much obliged for that, I reckon. Is that the only reason you came out here?"

She touched his arm again, this time gripping it more tightly. "No, I told you, I wanted to be sure you were all right."

"Maybe you were just checking up on me, seeing if I was up to any mischief."

"No. I trust you, Custis, whether anyone else does or not."

"What about that other fella, Baxter?"

In the dim light that filtered into the shadows under the

trees, Longarm saw Maggie shake her head. "I don't know him, don't know anything about him. I never saw him until today. The men seem to think he really is a famous shootist."

"Could be," Longarm said. "I don't know." He glanced toward the cabins. "I'm surprised the guard let you come out here."

"The men generally let me do whatever I want, unless Simon has given specific orders otherwise. To tell you the truth, Custis, I think they're all a little afraid of me." She laughed again. "They're afraid I'll accidentally blow them all up."

"Wouldn't want that to happen," Longarm said dryly.

"It's not likely to. I'm very careful."

"Did you use dynamite on those train tracks, or just nitroglycerine?"

"Just the soup," Maggie said. "I had an idea the vibrations of the rail as the train approached would set it off, and I was right."

"Four men died in that wreck, you know."

"I'm not surprised," she said coolly. "Does that make a difference . . . between you and me?"

For a moment, Longarm didn't say anything. Then he lied, "No. It doesn't make a difference."

"Good." Maggie leaned closer. "I'm glad to hear that." She brought her head next to his, and her lips found his mouth.

Longarm responded to the warm, wet, hungry sweetness of her kiss. Despite what he had told her, he would never feel the same about Maggie Flynn after discovering she was part of the gang that was responsible for at least seven deaths and untold destruction. But right now he needed her.

Not in the physical sense, although truth to tell, his shaft was beginning to harden as she slipped her tongue into his mouth and let it dart around hotly. He needed her because she was on his side. If he was going to have a chance to survive his stint in the gang until he discovered the identity

127

of the inside man at the Mint, if he was going to be able to bring Dugan and the others to justice, then he would need someone who believed in him, someone who would support him in case of any trouble. Maggie was the only possibility.

So for now, he would play along with her. It wouldn't be that difficult. She was still one of the most sensuous women he had encountered recently. She moved one of her hands down to his groin and massaged the long, thick pole of flesh that had stiffened until it was trapped uncomfortably in his trousers.

Longarm cupped her left breast, molding the pear-shaped mound in his fingers, feeling the hard button of the nipple prodding against his palm through the fabric of the man's shirt she wore. Maggie broke the kiss and whispered, "I wish I hadn't had to leave Little Elm when I did. I wanted us to have some more nights like the last one."

"I guess that train couldn't wait," Longarm said.

"No, it couldn't." Maggie started tugging at the buttons of his shirt. "But that's over now. Now we can be together again." She spread his shirt open and her head swooped down so that she could tongue his right nipple.

Longarm said, "You know there's a fella on the porch watching us. . . ."

"I don't care," Maggie panted. "It's dark here under the trees. He can't really see anything."

That was true, Longarm supposed. The guard would have spotted him in the moonlight if he had tried to leave the place where he'd spread his bedroll, but as long as he and Maggie stayed where they were, the watcher couldn't tell what they were doing. The man might guess, but that was as far as it would go.

"I'll be very quiet," Maggie whispered.

Longarm hoped he would be able to say the same thing. He shifted around so that his back was against the trunk of the tree, and extended his legs in front of him. He had barely gotten his belt unbuckled and his trousers unbut-

128

toned when Maggie began tugging them down his thighs. Longarm lifted his hips slightly so that she could pull down the long underwear at the same time. His erection bobbed up, free of its tight confines, and Maggie breathed, "Oh, yes," as she wrapped both hands around it.

Neither of them was in any mood to drag things out this time. After squeezing his shaft for a moment, Maggie hurriedly unfastened her own trousers and lowered them, then kicked them off completely. Still wearing her boots and the man's shirt, she straddled Longarm, planting a knee on each side of his hips. He reached out and placed his hand between her legs. His middle finger found the slick wetness of her core and slipped inside her, but the intimate caress was only momentary. When he slid his finger back out, she reached down and grasped his pole to aim it at her opening as she lowered herself. As soon as the head of his shaft had nudged its way between the folds of her feminine flesh, she practically lunged at him, burying him inside her to the hilt.

She had promised to be quiet, but the sudden sensation must have been too much. Longarm heard the beginnings of a keening cry welling up in her throat, so he kissed her, trapping her open mouth with his own so that the passionate wail could not escape. He wrapped his arms around her waist and hung on as her hips began bouncing up and down in a frenzy.

Her body molded so tightly to his that the two of them might as well have been one. She panted, "Yes, yes!" against his mouth. She was doing most of the work, but Longarm had to hang on to her because her hips were moving so fast.

In only a few minutes, he felt his climax percolating. That was probably all right with Maggie, because she had already been gripped by a pair of the shuddering spasms that marked her own culmination. Knowing there was no point in holding off, Longarm thrust up with his hips as she drove at him. He was buried as far in her as he could go, even though she gasped, "Deeper! Deeper!"

Longarm began to spurt inside her, showering the clutching, heated walls of her core with a flood of his scalding seed. Maggie buried her face against his shoulder and whimpered as she shook violently in the throes of yet another climax. Longarm threw his head back and held his breath until his own climax was finally over.

Maggie sagged against him, all her bones and muscles seemingly having turned to jelly. He cradled her there, and after a moment reached up to stroke her hair with a hand that trembled slightly. His brain was too blasted by passion to come up with any coherent thoughts.

Eventually, though, he caught his breath and regained at least some of his senses. He became aware that Maggie was talking.

". . . wonderful," she was saying. "I never . . . oh, Lord, Custis . . . I came so hard my teeth are tingling."

His softening shaft gave a little jump inside her that made her catch her breath. He chuckled tiredly. "I don't recollect anybody ever saying that to me before," he said.

"You never met anybody like me before."

That was certainly true enough, he thought. As far as he knew, none of his other lady friends had ever gone around blowing things up.

He frowned at that thought's unwanted intrusion. But it was too late. The moment was spoiled, and maybe that was good. He needed to remember just who and what Maggie Flynn was.

She lifted her hips so that he slid out of her. "I have to get back," she said. "Good night."

"Good night, Maggie."

"Don't worry about anything," she said as she pulled her trousers back on. "I'm sure Simon's going to decide to cooperate with you. And in the meantime . . . well, he's going to be gone for several days, he said. We'll have that time together, Custis."

"Yeah," Longarm said, hoping his voice didn't sound as hollow as he suddenly felt.

130

She leaned over, brushed a kiss across his mouth, and said again, "Good night." She got to her feet and started to slip away in the darkness, then paused abruptly and turned back to him. "Custis . . ." she said.

"What is it, Maggie?"

"I love you, Custis."

Then she was gone before he could say anything, flitting away into the night like a shadow.

Longarm sat there in silence for a long time, wishing like hell Maggie hadn't said that.

Chapter 15

Longarm finally got to sleep that night, but when he woke up the next morning, he was still tired. It was the smell of bacon cooking and coffee brewing that roused him. He sat up, rubbed his eyes, and looked around the valley.

The sky was orange-gray in the east, a harbinger of the approach of dawn. A couple of men were in the corral, tending to the gang's horses. As Longarm glanced torward the main cabin, he saw Maggie step out onto the porch and lift her arms over her head as she stretched like a cat. The movement lifted her breasts against her shirt, and Longarm couldn't help but think of what had happened the night before.

He reminded himself yet again not to allow that to color his judgment. No matter what had happened—no matter what Maggie had *said* the night before—she was still a killer and a bank robber.

Movement caught Longarm's eye, and he looked over to see Dan Boyd sauntering toward him. Boyd lifted a hand in greeting. "Morning, Custis," he said. "I see we both survived the night."

"Did you think we wouldn't?" Longarm asked.

"The thought crossed my mind," Boyd said dryly. "For

all I knew, Dugan gave his men orders to come out here and gun us as soon as he left."

"The same thing occurred to me," Longarm admitted. He paused, glancing around the camp. None of the outlaws were close by, and for a moment Longarm considered telling Boyd who he really was. If Boyd was another lawman, as Longarm suspected, that would get things out in the open between them so they could work together.

If, however, Boyd was actually the gunman he claimed to be, for Longarm to reveal that he was a star packer would likely be a death sentence. He would play things close to the vest for a while longer, Longarm decided.

Boyd didn't seem to be in a hurry to leave as Longarm stood up and gathered his bedroll. He propped a shoulder against a free trunk and said, "I reckon you're the first journalist I ever ran into who had a hankering to become a desperado."

"I figure I might even write a book about the gang," Longarm said. He was getting in deeper and deeper with this lie, and a part of him wished he had never started it. But it was too late to change things now, so all he could do was brazen it out.

"E. E. Polk. Wasn't that the name you said you use when you write?"

"That's right," Longarm said with a frown. What was Boyd up to?

"I read *Harper's Weekly* from time to time. Seems I've seen that name on some of the articles."

Damn it, Longarm thought. If Boyd started questioning him about stories that Polk had written in the past, there was no way Longarm could bluff his way through it. Why did Boyd have to be such a well-read son of a bitch?

He was saved from any further prying by Maggie's call from the porch. "Come on in and have some breakfast, you two."

Boyd turned toward the cabin with a grin and tugged on the brim of his black hat. "Thanks, ma'am. It smells mighty good." He looked back over his shoulder at Longarm. "Coming, Custis?"

"Yeah." Longarm wished Boyd would quit calling him by his real name. None of the members of the gang were outlaws Longarm had run across before, but some of them might have heard of a U.S. deputy marshal named Custis. Gossip was rife along the owlhoot trail, just like everywhere else in the world.

There were three men with Maggie in the main cabin when Longarm and Boyd entered, including the two who had been out at the corral a few minutes earlier. Longarm supposed the other members of the gang were standing watch at the tunnel and atop the cliff. The previous evening, things had been too tense for introductions, but Maggie took care of that now. As she placed plates of bacon and biscuits in front of the men, she said to Longarm and Boyd, "Meet Ed and Deke Chester and Jim Kimmel."

Longarm knew right away which ones were the Chester brothers. They were both rangy and dark-haired, and had prominent jaws covered with blue-black beard stubble. Kimmel was older, shorter, and stockier with a freckled face and tufts of sandy hair sticking out from under his hat. When he sat down at the table and thumbed back the battered Stetson, he revealed a balding scalp that was just as freckled as the rest of him. All three of the outlaws grunted greetings to the two newcomers. They didn't seem overly friendly, but at least they weren't threatening to kill Longarm and Boyd.

"Bob Hardaway and Luke Sims are standing guard," Maggie went on. "You've already met Luke. You'll meet Bob later." She seemed determined to keep things as civil, even pleasant, as possible.

"I'm glad to meet all you boys," Boyd said cheerfully as he sat down and pulled one of the plates in front of him. "I'm looking forward to working with you."

Longarm sat down too, and asked, "When's that going to be?"

Kimmel looked intently at him. "Don't get too nosy," he advised. "When Simon wants you to know something, he'll tell you."

"Yeah," one of the Chester brothers agreed. "Until then, askin' questions is a good way to get in trouble."

Longarm shrugged. "Thanks for the warning."

"It's not a warning," the other Chester brother said. "Just a fact."

Maggie brought a coffeepot from the stove, gripping the handle with a thick piece of leather to protect her hand, and began pouring the strong black brew in cups. "There's no need for anyone to get upset," she said, frowning at the three outlaws.

"No one's upset," Boyd said. He picked up one of the cups and sipped the coffee. "We're all friends here."

"Yeah," Kimmel grunted, not sounding the least bit sincere.

Longarm wanted to put things on a little better footing. He said, "Any of you boys like to play poker?"

The Chester brothers perked up right away. One of them said, "We like a good game of cards."

"So do I," Longarm said. "What say after breakfast we play a few hands? Since all we've got to do is wait, after all."

Kimmel nodded. "Might be a good idea at that." Like all poker players, he and the Chesters were interested by the idea of fresh meat.

With the atmosphere eased a bit, breakfast proceeded, and when it was finished and Maggie was cleaning up the dishes, Kimmel broke out a greasy pack of cards. He shuffled them, then since Boyd was sitting next to him, offered the deck to him for the cut. Boyd did so and handed it back, and Kimmel started to deal.

That was the beginning of a marathon game that lasted, with a few breaks, all day and into the night. Longarm played cautiously, winning an occasional hand, losing a few more, and folding frequently. The pots were never very big, and that was good because nobody was likely to get mad over losing a few dollars. The important thing was that Kimmel and the Chester brothers relaxed. The talk around the table was mostly of places they had been and people they had known, for the most part gamblers and thieves and whores. When Kimmel and Deke Chester left at midday to relieve Hardaway and Sims, the other two outlaws returned to the cabin and immediately took their places in the game. Obviously, Kimmel and Deke had told Hardaway and Sims that the two strangers were all right after all.

Longarm could tell that Maggie was bored. He was a little surprised she had not returned to Little Elm with Dugan when he went back to his masquerade as a respectable citizen and hotel owner. Perhaps she had meant to. Longarm couldn't help but wonder if she had stayed behind because he was here. Maybe that was a little immodest on his part, but otherwise why wouldn't Maggie have gone back to her role as schoolmarm and widow of the local bad man?

It could be she was just tired of that, Longarm speculated. The pose had to be difficult for her, feeling as she did about the town's reaction to her husband's conviction.

The card players took a couple of breaks to eat and change guards, and then the game finally wound to a close late in the evening. Longarm estimated he was up about twenty dollars. Not much to show for a day's work, but the day's real payoff wasn't financial. It was getting the outlaws to trust him and feel easy around him and Boyd. That had certainly been accomplished.

"No offense, boys," Luke Sims said as the game broke up, "but Simon told us to keep an eye on you until he got back, so I reckon that's what we'll have to do."

"Perfectly understandable," Boyd replied. "It takes a while before you know if a fella will do to ride the river with."

Kimmel had returned from his stint of sentry duty. He grinned and said, "Don't worry about that. Simon'll come up with some way for you gents to prove we can trust you."

Longarm didn't much like the sound of that. There was nothing he could do now, though, except wait.

And wonder if Maggie was going to pay him another visit tonight.

She did, and she was just as passionate as she had been the night before. Longarm fretted a bit that the other men would be jealous because Maggie was evidently intent on screwing him blind, but then what she was doing to him caught up to his thoughts and he found himself pumping her full of his seed again for the second time that night.

He would worry about everything else in the morning, he told himself.

The second day passed much like the first. Longarm, Boyd, and the other men spent it playing cards and shooting the breeze about a variety of things. Longarm had done some cowboying in Texas and along the cattle trails when he was just a gangling youngster, fresh from West-by-God-Virginia after the Late Unpleasantness had come to a close, so he concentrated on yarns from those days.

Late in the afternoon, Bob Hardaway asked, "How in Hades did you go from bein' a cowpuncher to bein' a reporter?"

"Well, a fella has lots of time to think about things while he's pushing steers up to the railhead," Longarm said. "I decided I didn't want to eat dust all my life. Picked up a copy of *Harper's* in Dodge City one day, read through it, and told myself I could do that. I wrote up a story about the Chisholm Trail and mailed it to 'em, and they wrote back and said they wanted to buy it." Longarm spread his hands. "It was as simple as that."

Deke Chester shook his head. "I wouldn't want to spend my days sittin' in some dark little room scribblin' stuff. I'd go loco in a hurry if I was to try to do that."

"So would I," his brother Ed agreed. "Give me somethin' decent where you're out in the fresh air."

137

Yeah, Longarm thought, something decent like robbing banks.

Maggie didn't come to his bedroll under the trees that night. Longarm stayed awake late, waiting for her, but the lamp went out in the main cabin and she never showed up. He finally dozed off, not quite sure whether to be disappointed or relieved.

Maggie acted friendly toward him the next morning, so Longarm didn't think she was angry with him. When he finally caught a moment alone with her, he said, "I sort of expected to see you again last night."

She glanced around, saw that none of the other men were within earshot, and said, "I didn't think it would be a good idea to come to you every night. I don't want any of the others getting the wrong idea."

Longarm didn't figure anybody had the wrong idea; the outlaw standing guard on the porch had seen her visiting him, and Longarm was certain the owlhoots had talked among themselves about what was going on. While none of them seemed jealous, there was no telling what Simon Dugan would do when he returned from Little Elm and was informed about Longarm and Maggie. Dugan hadn't seemed to mind that he and Maggie had a business partnership instead of a romantic one, but that might change.

Dugan's return came about sooner than anyone had expected. He rode back into the hidden valley about midday. Ed Chester was standing guard atop the cliff when he fired two shots from his Winchester, then a third after a short pause. Longarm, Boyd, and Jim Kimmel were sitting on the porch, Longarm and Kimmel smoking cheroots, when the shots sounded. Maggie came hurrying out of the cabin. "That's the signal to let us know Simon's coming in," she said.

"Reckon he's got something else lined up already?" Kimmel asked. "I didn't think that big job he was talkin' about was goin' to come off for a while yet."

Big job, Longarm thought. An even bigger job than the

138

derailment and robbery of the train carrying that outdated currency?

Kimmel's comment surprised Longarm a little. Three days ago, the outlaw would not have been so careless with his words around relative strangers, would not have dropped so much as a hint about the gang's future plans. That showed how much he had come to accept Longarm and Boyd in a relatively short time.

"I don't know," Maggie said in answer to Kimmel's question. "I guess we'll just have to wait and see."

Longarm knew she was right, but he was getting tired of waiting. He would almost welcome some trouble.

He still had not been away from the area around the cabins, so he didn't know exactly where the tunnel through the cliff came out. Dugan rode in from downstream, though, which was not surprising. Longarm had already figured out that the stream had most likely carved out the passage used by the gang. Dugan had changed out of his town suit and back into range clothes. Everyone except the two sentries, Ed Chester and Luke Sims, was waiting for him on the porch when he rode up.

"Well, if this ain't a handsome group," Dugan said with a grin as he reined in. "Maggie, darlin', how are you?"

"I'm fine, Simon," she replied. "How is everything in Little Elm?"

"As sleepy as ever. Goble just about has his blacksmith shop rebuilt. I reckon the town will recover."

"A shame," Maggie said, and as Longarm looked at her, he saw that she meant it.

"Indeed." Dugan swung down from the saddle and handed the reins to Deke Chester, who stepped down from the porch to take them. As he looked at Longarm and Boyd, Dugan went on. "And what about our two new members? Have they behaved themselves?"

"We've been gettin' along fine, Simon," Kimmel said. "No problems."

"Good. Come along inside, all of you. I've got something to show you."

Dugan went into the cabin first, followed by the others. He hung his hat on a nail and then went to the table, where a bottle of whiskey stood with the cork in it. Dugan picked it up, pulled the cork with his teeth, and spat it out into his other hand. He tilted the bottle to his lips and took a long swallow. When he lowered it, he wiped the back of his hand across his mouth and said, "It's a long, dry ride from Little Elm, my friends. But that cut the dust just fine."

He thumped the cork back into the neck of the bottle with the heel of his hand, then replaced it on the table. Reaching under his vest, he took a folded piece of paper from his shirt pocket and spread it out.

"Take a look," he invited the others. "It's a map of a town called Camden."

Longarm had heard of the place. It was just over the border in Colorado. He wasn't certain what Dugan's interest in Camden was, but he had a sneaking suspicion.

"The settlement is right in the middle of some rich ranch country," Dugan went on, "which means they've got a nice little bank there." His finger speared one of the squares on the map that represented buildings. "Right here, in fact."

Like the others, Longarm leaned over the table and studied the map. Someone had gone to a great deal of effort to draw it and place as many details about the town as possible on it. Each building was neatly labeled. The precision struck Longarm as military-like.

That was another bit of information to be filed away. This map could have come from Dugan's accomplice in the Mint, and the man could have some sort of army connection. That was assuming a lot of things not in evidence, as the lawyers put it, Longarm thought, but the theory was certainly possible.

"We goin' to hit this bank, Simon?" Kimmel asked.

Dugan nodded. "That we are. But not all of us."

"What do you mean?" Maggie asked.

"Deke and Luke are going to stay here," Dugan said. He looked straight at Longarm and Boyd. "But Polk and Baxter will be going along. If they want to join us, it's time for us to find out what these boyos are made of."

Chapter 16

Longarm had been expecting something like that ever since Dugan had made the comment about him and Boyd having to prove themselves. He kept his face impassive as Dugan looked across the table at him.

"Well?" the outlaw chief said after a moment. "What about it? Are you still in?"

"How much money do you think is in that bank?" Boyd asked. "That's the important question."

Dugan laughed. "Get right to the point, don't you, Baxter?"

"No reason not to," the black-hatted gunman replied.

"I figure we'll take at least seventy-five thousand out of there."

Boyd nodded and said, "That's a good payoff. I'm in."

"So am I," Longarm said.

"Being part of a bank robbery is a lot different than writing about it," Dugan said.

Longarm met his intent gaze with a cool, level stare of his own. "I know that. And I'm ready."

Dugan slapped a palm on the table, the sound sharp and loud in the close confines of the cabin. "All right, then. Look at the map, Maggie, and tell us where you'll put your little toys this time."

Maggie leaned over the table for several minutes, a wing of her blond hair falling forward over her face as she studied the unfolded paper. "Here," she finally said. "And here and here and here." She stabbed a finger at each of the buildings in turn. "All those buildings should be empty in the middle of the night, but the blasts will still cause so much havoc that no one will have time to come after us, if they even notice the bank's been robbed."

"Still the softhearted colleen," Dugan said with a grin. "You don't want to blow up anyone."

Maggie shrugged. "I don't see any point in killing when it's not necessary. I helped you derail that train, though, didn't I?"

"You certainly did, and did a fine job of it too. And profited by it handsomely."

Maggie changed the subject by saying, "Has anyone noticed that I'm gone from Little Elm?"

"Yes indeed. Brad Holcomb is mighty upset about it too. He's been haranguing Sheriff Kingman about it for days. But I have to say that the rest of the townspeople don't seem to be too concerned."

Maggie snorted in contempt. "They wouldn't be. I was nothing to them but a reminder of Tim."

"You got your revenge on them. They'll never forget those explosions, even though it looks like the town will survive." Dugan picked up the map, refolded it, and placed it in his pocket again. Turning to Longarm and Boyd, he said, "You'll get your guns back when we leave tomorrow. But until the job's over, we'll still be watching you."

"Fair enough," Boyd said. "Don't you think so, Polk?"

"Yeah," Longarm said. "That's fair." At least Boyd hadn't called him Custis that time, he thought.

The gang was riding out tomorrow, Dugan had said. It would take a day or so to reach Camden.

That meant Longarm had a couple of days to figure out how to stop them from blowing up half the town without revealing who he really was.

143

• • •

After breakfast the next morning, the outlaws gathered their gear, including enough supplies to last for several days, and saddled their horses. Longarm noticed that Maggie handled that chore for herself, even though any of the men probably would have been glad to do it for her. Clearly, she was determined to pull her own weight in the gang.

Dugan came to Longarm and Boyd and handed over their guns. Longarm slid the walnut-butted .44 back into the cross-draw rig. The familiar weight of the revolver in its holster felt good, and now that it was back, Longarm realized just how much he had missed it over the past few days.

Boyd hefted the pair of ivory-handled Colts in his hands, then twirled them and slipped them back into their holsters of scrolled black leather. It was another dude's trick, but with Boyd the move seemed natural. "What about our rifles?" he asked.

"You won't need them," Dugan said. "But we'll take them along, just in case."

Armed again, Longarm felt like a new man as he swung up into the saddle. His mind even seemed sharper, the wheels clicking over efficiently as he thought about the dilemma facing him. He didn't have an answer yet, but he was confident he would come up with one.

Leaving Deke Chester and Luke Sims behind to keep an eye on the hideout, the gang rode along the meandering little creek until it turned sharply toward a bluff with a steep rock face. Longarm saw the irregular black opening that marked the tunnel. The creek ran into it, filling the tunnel from one side to the other. The water was shallow, though, only a few inches deep, so the horses were able to splash through it easily.

The roof of the tunnel was low. All the riders had to bend over in the saddle except for Maggie, who was short enough so that the top of her hat just barely brushed the roof. Longarm, who was taller than any of the others, was beginning to find the riding stance uncomfortable by the time the group reached the other end of the passage. It was hidden behind some brush and a cluster of boulders that had fallen from the cliff above. When the riders emerged from the tunnel into the open air once more, Longarm straightened gratefully in his saddle.

Dugan headed west, following the line of the cliff, and the others trailed along with him. After half a day's ride, the cliff finally ended, and they were able to turn northwest. Soon, they were out of the rocky hills and back on the rolling prairie that filled so much of this part of the country.

Longarm found himself riding alongside Maggie. Whether that was by accident or design, he didn't know or care. They didn't talk much, but then none of the others did either. They were on serious business now; the chatter of the poker table was forgotten.

By nightfall, Longarm figured they were either back in Colorado or right on the border. They made a cold camp. Out here on the plains, a fire could be seen for a long way, and Dugan didn't want to risk that. Supper was jerky and biscuits brought from the hideout, washed down by water from their canteens.

"We'll get to Camden sometime tomorrow afternoon," Dugan said. "We'll lie low until it's dark. That'll give Maggie time to put together the explosives. Then we'll slip into the settlement when it's good and dark and plant the stuff. We'll be waiting at the bank when it goes off."

Longarm wondered how Maggie was carrying the nitroglycerine. He knew she had a dozen or so sticks of dynamite in her saddlebags, because he had seen her putting them there before they left the hideout. His other question was answered when she opened the top button of her shirt and drew out a good-sized glass vial that had been cradled in the soft valley between her breasts. The vial had a cork stopper in its neck and was suspended from a rawhide thong that was looped around Maggie's neck. Longarm thought about how he had ridden beside Maggie all day. If

145

that vial had somehow gotten itself a good hard jolt, there probably wouldn't have been enough left of Maggie, Longarm, or their horses for the rest of the gang to scrape up and bury. He understood now why the other men rode well away from her.

Maggie placed the vial carefully on the ground beside the spot where she spread her bedroll. Longarm said dryly, "You'd better not go to thrashing around in your sleep, Maggie."

"Don't worry," she assured him. "Nothing's going to happen."

"But you won't be minding if the rest of us keep our distance, will you, Maggie?" Dugan said with a chuckle.

"Go ahead," Maggie told him. She looked at Longarm and added, "You too."

He hesitated, then untied the thongs that held his soogans in a roll and spread them out near hers. "Right here's fine with me," he declared.

"A brave man," Boyd said. "But bravery doesn't always go hand in hand with wisdom."

Longarm glared at him. "You sleep where you want to, and I'll sleep where I want to."

Boyd held up his hands, palms out in a gesture of peace, and said, "I wouldn't dream of telling you where to sleep, friend."

"The dead don't dream," Dugan said.

Boyd glanced sharply at him. "What do you mean by that?"

Dugan shook his head. "Nothing. Just a bit of Irish philosophy."

"The only Irish philosophy I know is that old toast about being in Heaven a half hour before the Devil knows you're dead," Longarm said.

"The Devil always knows."

Longarm couldn't argue with that. Ol' Scratch seemed to keep pretty up to date on mankind's failings, sure enough.

146

Despite the presence of the vial of nitroglycerine on the ground nearby, Longarm slept fairly well. He was rested when the gang ate more jerky and biscuits for breakfast, then saddled up and rode out just before dawn the next morning. The nitroglycerine was back where it belonged, the thong around Maggie's neck and the vial nestled once more between her breasts.

Longarm was sure they had reached Colorado when he spotted a thin blue line on the horizon, barely visible to the naked eye. That was the mountains of the Front Range, he knew, almost unnoticeable at this distance unless someone was looking for them.

The gang was riding due north now. As Dugan had predicted, they reached the vicinity of Camden during the afternoon. Dugan led them down into some trees along a creek and then held up a hand to signal a halt.

"We'll wait here until after dark," he said. "We're off the regular trails. There shouldn't be anybody coming along to stumble over us."

The horses drank from the stream, then began grazing on the grass that grew along the bank. The men rested, Bob Hardaway and Ed Chester going so far as to stretch out on the ground and go to sleep. Jim Kimmel took a small block of wood from his pocket and began carving on it with a folding knife.

That left Dugan, Maggie, Longarm, and Boyd to pass the time by talking quietly. Longarm hoped this would give him an opportunity to learn more about the so-called "big job" Kimmel had mentioned back at the hideout.

Instead, though, Dugan talked at length about his childhood back in Ireland. He and his family had come to America in the early fifties, fleeing from the potato famine. Dugan had still been a boy at the time.

"I reckon that's why you sound more Irish at some times than at others," Longarm commented. "You've been over here long enough to lose the accent, but the way we were as youngsters never completely goes away."

"That's true," Dugan agreed. He looked at Boyd. "What about you, Baxter? Where are you from?"

"West Texas," Boyd answered without hesitation. "God's present to the rest of the world."

"Why would the Almighty give the rest of the world a lot of sand, rocks, scorpions, and rattlesnakes?" Longarm asked with a smile. "Wasn't it Phil Sheridan who once said that if he owned both Hell and Texas, he'd live in Hell and rent out Texas?"

"Sheridan was a Yankee," Boyd replied, as if that explained everything. And having met plenty of Texans in his life, Longarm supposed that it did.

Maggie took the dynamite from her saddlebags and divided it up, three sticks in each bundle. She lashed them together and then stowed them away again. Longarm watched her, then said, "I thought you used the nitroglycerine with that."

"I'll put a small vial with each bundle of dynamite," she replied. "But I don't fill those vials until I'm ready to place the explosives where they go."

Longarm nodded. "It must take a steady hand to pour that stuff from one vial to the other."

Dugan said, "Maggie has the steadiest hand of anybody I've ever seen, except maybe for Tim. He had a knack for handling that devil's soup. I think he could have juggled bottles of it without it ever going off."

"We'll never know about that, will we?" Maggie said quietly.

That reminder of Timothy Flynn's death had a sobering effect on the outlaws. They were fairly quiet as the sun slid below the horizon and the shadows of night began to gather.

Longarm stood near the horses and wished he could figure out a way to stop this from happening. He had been wracking his brain ever since the gang had left the hideout, but so far he hadn't come up with anything. If he declared himself as a lawman, he might be able to take the others by surprise and get the drop on them—especially if Dan Boyd was a fellow star packer, as Longarm suspected, and threw in with him.

But even if he succeeded in capturing the outlaws—something that could by no means be guaranteed—the inside man who had tipped off Dugan about the shipment of money would get away scot-free. Longarm thought about the men who had died in that crash, and he didn't like that option. But he didn't like the idea of putting the lives of innocent settlers in Camden at risk either.

Damned if he did, damned if he didn't. That just about summed it up, Longarm decided.

Then Maggie came up beside him and laid a hand on his arm. "Take a walk with me, Custis," she said in a low voice, low enough so that the others couldn't overhear.

Longarm looked at her in surprise. "Where are we going?"

"Down by the creek."

Longarm hesitated, then took the hand she held out to him. The moon had not yet risen, but there was enough light from the stars for them to see where they were going as they made their way through the trees and along the creek. Longarm let Maggie take the lead, and she didn't stop until they were about a hundred yards away from the others.

She halted then and turned to him, coming into his arms and lifting her face to his for a kiss. Longarm obliged, pressing his mouth to hers for a long moment that grew steadily more passionate. When Maggie finally broke the kiss, Longarm said quietly, "I'm surprised Dugan let you come out here with me like this."

"Simon knows he can't order me around like he does the others. Without me he's just a two-bit bank robber."

"That nitroglycerine makes all the difference, doesn't it?"

"I suppose so." Maggie took a step back and reached up to grasp the thong around her neck. Carefully, she lifted it over her head. "But I'm tired of carrying it right now. I

149

want to put it aside. I want to put everything aside and just be with you, Custis."

Longarm's jaw tightened. The way he felt about Maggie Flynn was a mass of contradictions, but he was certain of one thing. He had to stop what was about to happen, and for the first time, he though he had a glimmering of how to do it.

"I want to be with you too," he said.

Maggie held out the vial of nitroglycerine. "Hold this."

Longarm cupped both hands together, and she lowered the vial into them. He stood absolutely still as she quickly stripped off her shirt, peeled her trousers down her legs, and dropped the clothes in a pile on the ground. Naked, she turned to him and held out her hands.

"I'll take it back now."

Longarm was barely breathing as he handed the vial to her. She bent and placed it on top of her clothes.

"It should be safe there," she said as she straightened. She stepped closer to Longarm and reached for the buttons of his shirt. "Let's get you out of these clothes."

The grass was thick and soft on the creek bank, and the trees shielded them from the view of the others, though Longarm didn't doubt for a minute that Dugan, at least, knew what was going on. In a matter of moments, he was as bare as Maggie was, and as he embraced her, she reached down and closed her hand around his shaft. They both sank to the ground.

For several minutes, they lay there kissing and fondling each other. Then Maggie abruptly rolled off Longarm and positioned herself on her hands and knees. Her breathing was harsh and fast with need as she looked over her shoulder at him and said, "Do it to me from behind again."

Longarm's organ was achingly stiff, more than ready to be plunged into the wet and waiting female flesh. He moved behind her, then grasped her hips and eased her a little to one side. "This is better," he said. "You comfortable?"

"I'm fine," she gasped. "Just put it in me!"

He brought the head of his shaft to her opening and teased her for a second with it, running it along the lips and feeling the moisture that welled from him mixing with the dew that came from her. Maggie's head lowered until it was resting on her crossed arms. She moaned.

Longarm wanted her as excited as possible, so he leaned over and reached around her to cup both breasts. At the same time, he slowly brought his hips forward, so that the thick pole jutting out from his groin eased into her. Her core spread open to accept him, and another moan escaped from her lips as he filled her.

Longarm wanted to groan himself as her muscles clenched on him in a hot grip. Moving with maddening deliberation, he slid back, then forward again. Maggie grew wetter and wetter, so that Longarm could hear the faint liquid sounds made by their joining. It took a great deal of willpower on his part to keep from driving hard into her and increasing his pace.

It took even more willpower and concentration to reach out and grasp the vial of nitroglycerine, then lift it off the pile of discarded clothing.

Chapter 17

Truth to tell, Longarm had made love in some pretty bizarre circumstances in the past. But he couldn't remember ever being in a situation quite as odd—or dangerous—as this one. He had to keep Maggie excited and aroused enough so that she wouldn't notice what he was doing, but at the same time he couldn't allow himself to get so carried away that he wasn't paying attention to the devil's brew in his hand. His hips came forward again so that his shaft plumbed her depths.

"That feels so good, Custis!" she groaned.

Damned right it did, Longarm thought. His thigh muscles trembled a little from the strain of crouching behind her.

His free hand stroked her back while he gingerly tried to work free the cork stopper in the neck of the vial.

Maggie's hips started to buck back against him, and Longarm's eyes widened as he saw the liquid in the vial begin to slosh around. He stiffened his arm, letting his body absorb the impact of Maggie's thrusts. His lips drew back from his teeth in a grimace as he struggled to ease the stopper out.

It came free with a faint "pop." Longarm barely heard the noise, so he figured it was unlikely Maggie had, considering the worked-up state she was in. Moving slowly and carefully, he lowered the vial to the ground and then eased it over. The nitroglycerine began to run out.

"Custis, what . . . what are you doing?"

Longarm had a bad couple of seconds before he realized that Maggie wasn't talking about how he was emptying the vial. She was just expressing her emotions. She went on. "What are you doing to me? I can't stand it, it's so wonderful!"

Longarm lifted the vial and held it close to his face, studying it in the starlight as he continued sliding his shaft in and out of Maggie. Some of the nitroglycerine was still clinging to the sides of the glass container, but there wasn't much of it left.

"Hang on tight," he growled. Then, with a flick of his hips, he drove powerfully into her, bringing a sharp cry of lust from her. He kept it up, thrusting hard, so hard that Maggie had no choice except to scoot forward a little.

Now he could reach the edge of the creek. He dipped the vial into the water and brought it back up full, then switched it to his other hand so he could feel around in the darkness for the stopper. There was another bad moment as he couldn't find it at first, but then his fingers fell on it and snatched it up. He was humping like a son of a bitch now, giving Maggie everything he had. He jammed the stopper back into the neck of the vial, then shook the container hard several times to fling away any drops of water clinging to it outside. A grunt of effort escaped from him as he tossed the vial back onto the pile of Maggie's clothes.

Then, at long last, he was able to give himself over to the sensations that had been trying to overwhelm him. He grabbed her hips, pulled back hard against him, and thrust into her with such force that he was a little surprised she didn't come up off the ground. Maggie whimpered and convulsed as Longarm began spurting inside her.

A timeless moment later, as their climaxes passed, both of them slumped forward onto the ground. Maggie was lying facedown in the grass, and Longarm was on top of her. He tried to support his weight on his elbows and knees so he wouldn't crush her, but he was too wrung out by everything that had happened during the past few minutes.

He had heard lovemaking called the little death. If he had dropped that vial at the wrong time, he reflected, he and Maggie would have experienced the big death.

But he hadn't dropped it, and now, if Maggie didn't discover the switch, even if he was unable to prevent the explosions that would rock Camden tonight, at least maybe they wouldn't be so devastating. Longarm wasn't through, but at least he had taken the first step.

"Oh . . . oh, my," Maggie said raggedly. "I never . . . I just never felt anything like that before, Custis."

Longarm moved off her, and she rolled over so that she could look up at him.

"You're going to stay with us, aren't you?" she asked.

He was having a little trouble catching his breath. "I reckon," he managed to say. "If Dugan will let me."

"You won't have to worry about writing anymore," Maggie went on. "After the next job after this, we'll all be so rich none of us will ever have to worry about working again. Or robbing banks either."

Longarm stretched out beside her and propped himself on an elbow. "Sounds like Dugan's got something mighty big planned," he said. As long as Maggie was willing to talk, he was willing to listen.

"The biggest," she said. "Bigger than that train robbery, bigger than any robbery that's ever been attempted."

Longarm chuckled. "You make it sound like he's planning to hit the Mint."

Maggie looked up at him and said solemnly, "That's exactly what we're going to do. We're going to rob the Denver Mint."

By the time they were dressed and had returned to the camp a few minutes later, Longarm didn't know much more than he had when Maggie made that startling revelation. She had

154

gone close-mouthed after that, and as they were dressing, he could tell that she was worried she had already said too much.

Even without the details, Longarm could make some educated guesses about the plan. He knew how well the Mint was guarded. Even with a man on the inside working with the gang, it would take one hell of a distraction to enable the robbers to get inside.

Setting off explosions all over downtown Denver would probably do it, Longarm figured.

"You about ready to go, Maggie?" Dugan asked when the two of them returned to camp.

Maggie nodded. "I'm ready. Let's get this over with."

The moon had still not risen, so it would be good and dark as the robbers approached the settlement and made their way in. Longarm mounted up and fell in with the others, riding slowly and quietly toward Camden. Lights were still burning in a few of the buildings, most likely the saloons, but for the most part the town was dark and quiet.

The riders stuck to the back alleys, reining in several times at Dugan's signal as they circled the settlement. At each stop, Maggie slipped from her saddle and took one of the bundles of dynamite out of her saddlebags. She also took a glass vial with her each time, smaller than the one she carried around her neck. It would take only a small amount of the nitroglycerine to dramatically increase the destructive power of the explosions.

Longarm sat tensely on his horse at each of these stops while Maggie disappeared into the shadows between the buildings. He was worried that she would notice something different about the contents of the vial she wore around her neck. Pure nitroglycerine was clear like water, but it was slightly oily.

There was nothing he could do about it now, he told himself. He had taken the risk of replacing the nitro in order to cut down on the damage to the town in case he couldn't stop the explosions entirely. He hadn't given up on that hope yet.

He glanced over at Dan Boyd. The black-hatted gunman's face was partially in shadow, and the part Longarm could see was totally impassive.

Longarm hoped his own features were equally lacking in expression. If anyone had been able to discern his thoughts at that moment, he would be in trouble.

Maggie came back from planting the last of her lethal little bundles. Each of them had had a long fuse attached to it, Longarm knew, although the fuses grew shorter with each bundle. That way they would all explode about the same time. Maggie must have done a lot of experimenting in order to learn how to cut the fuse to the precise lengths she needed.

"Ready?" Dugan asked.

"Ready," Maggie replied as she swung up into her saddle. "Let's head for the bank."

The riders moved out, walking their horses toward the rear of the building that housed the town's bank. If no one noticed the sputtering sparks of the burning fuses, in a few minutes Camden's peaceful night would be ripped apart by a series of blasts. Longarm's jaw clenched tightly as he thought about the devastation awaiting the town. He tried to weigh that against the chance to expose the gang's inside man at the Mint.

"Same as before," Dugan said quietly as they reined in behind the bank. "We bust through the back door and Maggie blows the safe with that soup of hers. Then we ride out while everybody in town's running around trying to figure out if it's the end of the world."

That was what it would seem like, all right, Longarm thought. In the minds of its citizens, apocalypse would come to Camden tonight.

And he had to stop it. Suddenly, he knew that. He couldn't risk the lives of innocent people, not even to expose the villainy of whoever in Denver was working with Dugan on the plan to rob the Mint.

"Damn it!" Jim Kimmel burst out. "Where's Baxter?"

Dugan twisted around in his saddle to stare at Kimmel, as did everyone else in the group. "What?" Dugan demanded. "Baxter's gone?"

It was true, Longarm realized. The big stallion was still there, but its saddle was empty. Boyd, or Baxter, or whatever the hell his name was, had slipped away from the gang so quietly, fading into the deep shadows, that no one had noticed him leaving. The man's dark clothing had undoubtedly made it easier.

Longarm knew an opportunity when he saw one. He said quickly, "I'll find him," and started to wheel his horse around.

"Jim!" Dugan snapped. For a heartbeat, Longarm thought the outlaw leader was going to try to stop him. But then Dugan went on. "Go with Polk. Find that son of a bitch before he ruins everything!"

Kimmel grunted in acknowledgment of the order and turned his horse. He fell in beside Longarm, and the two of them rode back the way they had come, retracing their route through the alleys to the last place the gang had stopped so Maggie could plant a bundle of explosives.

"I never trusted that bastard," Kimmel said harshly as he and Longarm rounded a corner. "He's double-crossing us for some reason."

"I reckon," Longarm said. At the same time, he slipped his Colt from its holster with his left hand, reversed it, and whipped his arm out so that the butt of the gun slammed into the side of Kimmel's head.

The outlaw grunted again and fell loosely out of the saddle. Longarm reined in and jumped down from his horse. At the very least, Kimmel had been knocked out by the blow, just as Longarm had hoped.

Longarm flipped the Colt around and transferred it to his right hand, holding it ready as he knelt beside Kimmel and checked the man's pulse. Kimmel was still alive, Longarm discovered, but he was out cold. Longarm yanked Kimmel's bandanna off, whipped it into a tight roll, and tied it around the man's head so that it was tight in his mouth. If Kimmel regained consciousness, it would take him a few moments to pull the makeshift gag loose and let out a yell.

A little time was all that Longarm was asking for right now.

He stood up and grabbed his horse's reins. Kimmel's mount had wandered on down the alley, and Longarm let it go. Leading his horse, he trotted toward the spot where he hoped to find Boyd.

He had just passed a dark alcove when he heard a faint noise behind him, the scrape of boot leather on dirt. Longarm dropped the reins and started to turn, but the cold ring of metal that was pressed suddenly to the back of his neck stopped him.

"Don't move," Dan Boyd breathed. "I don't want to kill you, but I will if I have to."

The tension gripping Longarm eased a little—but only a little. He was still all too aware of the fuses burning in the darkness of the sleeping town.

"Take it easy, old son," Longarm said. "I got a hunch we're on the same side."

"Longarm?"

Longarm caught his breath. He was surprised to hear his nickname come from Boyd, who must have noted the reaction because he went on. "Yeah, I thought it was you. Custis Long. U.S. deputy marshal out of Denver, works for Billy Vail."

"How do you know that?"

"Because you're the only Custis I ever heard of, and I used to be a marshal too, before I retired and went to work as a railroad detective."

Well, that explained a lot, Longarm thought, but he and Boyd didn't have time right now to fill each other in on their life stories. Still, he couldn't resist saying, "Glad to meet you . . . Boyd."

"How did you—" The gun barrel went away from Longarm's neck. "I reckon we can hash that out later. Come on, we've got to stop that dynamite and nitroglycerine from going off."

"The soup's nothing but water," Longarm said as he turned toward Boyd. "I switched it earlier."

Boyd chuckled as he broke into a trot. "I won't ask you how you distracted Miz Flynn."

The two men, one a federal star packer and the other a former rider for Uncle Sam, hurried along the alley. Longarm wasn't exactly sure where Maggie had planted each of the bundles, but he hoped he and Boyd could find all of them in time.

Boyd ducked into a familiar lane that ran alongside a building. Longarm followed, and halfway down the dark, narrow space, they spotted a faint orange glow. Longarm kicked aside a rotten crate, exposing the bundle of dynamite with the vial of what was supposed to be nitroglycerine attached to it. The fuse leading to the fulminate of mercury caps on the dynamite was still about a foot long.

Longarm's boot heel came down on the sputtering tip of the fuse and ground it out. He leaned over and jerked what was left of the fuse loose from the dynamite, just as a precaution.

"Better leave it there for now," Boyd said. "We've got to get to the others."

They weren't going to make it. Longarm knew that now. With the explosives all set to go off at about the same time, there could be only a minute or so left. But maybe he and Boyd could stop at least one more of the blasts.

They were closer to the main street of Camden, so they went that way, cutting across at a dead run toward another alley. Down the street, a solitary rider saw them and called out curiously to them, but Longarm and Boyd ignored him. They sprinted down another alley, trying to remember the map they had studied along with the rest of the gang and pinpoint the location of the next batch of explosives.

Boyd found them, concealed in a side doorway that was recessed from the alley. He jerked the fuse loose and tossed it aside, where Longarm stomped it out. This time the fuse was only six inches long.

"Come on," Boyd said urgently. "This way."

Suddenly, Longarm knew that Boyd was going in the wrong direction. He wasn't sure why, but his instincts told him to head in a different direction. He grabbed Boyd's arm and said, "No, it's over there."

Boyd hesitated, but only for an instant. "We'll split up," he said.

Longarm nodded curtly and broke into a run. Maybe this way they could reach the remaining bundles of dynamite in time.

And maybe this way they'd both get blown to bits too. But that was the chance they had to take.

Longarm flung himself around a corner and paused, looking back and forth. The building to his left was a blacksmith shop, or so he thought. To his right was a hardware store. Both of them were closed and dark at this hour of the night. Either would have made a good target for Maggie. She had planted explosives in one of them, Longarm was fairly sure of that, because he was certain she had come down this alley.

But which building?

The hardware store had a side door; the blacksmith shop didn't. Longarm let that fact make up his mind for him and darted toward the door. He grabbed the knob, twisted it, jerked the unlocked door open. He plunged into the hardware store, seeing the shelves and counters looming around him in the shadows. His eyes frantically searched the darkness for the telltale glow of sparks from the burning fuse.

Nothing. He dashed along the aisles, running into things and barking his shins painfully. Still no sign of the dynamite. He turned toward the rear door, which he had left open behind him. . . .

Just as he faced the door, he saw the bright red flash that filled it, heard the roar that slammed into his ears like a pair of giant fists, felt the hammering force that knocked him backward. Longarm had time to realize that he was flying through the air—then he crashed into something.

After that, blackness claimed him, and he didn't know a thing.

Chapter 18

The night was on fire. That was the only explanation for the angry red streaks shooting through the darkness.

After a few moments, Longarm realized that the darkness was in his head, and so was the hellish glare of the fire. He groaned, lifted his head, and managed to force his eyes open.

Wrong again, he thought. The flames weren't figments of his imagination after all. They were all around him, and as he rolled onto his side and began to cough from the smoke that filled his lungs, a burning beam from the ceiling crashed to the floor of the hardware store only a few feet away. Longarm covered his head with his arms as blazing debris showered around him.

The part of his brain that was still functioning reasonably well knew that the blacksmith shop next door had blown up. Even without the nitroglycerine, the dynamite was powerful enough to have done considerable damage and started a fire, a fire that had obviously spread to the hardware store.

Figuring that out was all well and good, he told himself, but the important thing now was to get out of there before the blaze claimed his life. He pushed himself onto his hands and knees, still wracked by coughs, and then lurched up onto his feet.

The flames were all around him, which made it difficult to orient himself. Where was the damned door? he asked himself. Of course it didn't really matter, because the whole wall on that side of the store had been caved in by the explosion next door, he saw as he squinted against the glare and peered through the fire. He started stumbling toward it, knowing he was going to be burned but not seeing any other way out.

A hand shot out from behind him and gripped his arm hard. "This way!" a voice shouted hoarsely. "Come this way!"

Longarm looked over his shoulder and saw Dan Boyd. Boyd was tugging him toward the opposite side of the store, and when Longarm saw the broken window over there, he knew how Boyd had gotten in. Boyd was right: The fire wasn't as bad over there yet. If Longarm hadn't been so stunned from the blast, he would have seen that for himself.

He staggered toward the broken window, guided by Boyd at first, but regaining more of his strength with every step. When they reached that side of the store, Longarm lifted his voice to call over the crackle and roar of the conflagration, "Go ahead! I can make it!"

"You first, Long!" Boyd insisted.

Longarm knew that arguing would just cost them both more time. He threw a leg over the sill, not worrying about the broken glass that clawed at him as he tumbled through the window, and fell to the dirt of the alley outside. Boyd landed beside him a second later. The two men scrambled to their feet and ran out of the alley.

The blacksmith shop had been mostly leveled by the blast, Longarm saw as they emerged on the main street, and the fire in the hardware store was burning so strongly that there would be no chance of saving the building. Up the street, another blaze sent flames leaping high in the sky and lit up the night. Boyd hadn't reached his destination in time to prevent the second explosion.

But evidently only two blasts had rocked the town. Longarm looked around and asked, "Where's the bank?" He was still a little groggy.

Boyd pointed. "Over there!"

Suddenly, he grabbed Longarm's shoulder, jerked him around, and threw a wicked right-hand punch that cracked hard into Longarm's jaw. Taken by surprise, Longarm staggered and almost fell.

"Fight back!" Boyd hissed.

Longarm heard the pound of hoofbeats. Several riders charged out of the alley beside the bank, and Longarm realized they were Simon Dugan, Maggie Flynn, and the other marauders. Kimmel had regained consciousness and rejoined them again, Longarm saw from the corner of his eye as he slammed a straight right into Boyd's face, knocking the railroad detective back a step.

"Find Billy Vail, chief marshal in Denver," Longarm grated. "Dugan's going to hit the Mint."

Boyd recovered his balance and slugged Longarm again. "I'll have guards waiting," he said.

"I'll try to find out the name of the inside man." Longarm blocked Boyd's next punch and threw another one of his own. "I'll give the signal to move in!"

"Got it. Now shoot me!" Boyd said.

Longarm whipped his Colt from its holster and fired. The slug sizzled past Boyd's left side, missing him by no more than six inches and plowing into the street behind him. Boyd folded up anyway, crossing his arms over his belly and doubling over as he pretended to have been hit. He fell loosely into the dust, looking for all the world like a man who had just been gut-shot.

Longarm turned away from the fallen Boyd and bellowed, "Maggie!" He waved his gun over his head.

They were already galloping toward him. That was good, Longarm thought, because it meant they had seen him apparently gun down Boyd. Longarm wasn't sure how he was going to explain about knocking out Kimmel, but if there was still a slim chance to hold on to his place in the gang, he intended to take it.

For a second, he thought Dugan was going to ride him down. But then the outlaw swerved and extended his right hand. Longarm jammed his gun back in its holster and reached up to grab Dugan's wrist as the outlaw's horse swept past him. He leaped at the same time.

The jolt wrenched painfully at Longarm's shoulder, but he hung on and flung his left leg over the back of Dugan's racing mount. He clutched Dugan around the waist and settled down on the horse's back just behind the saddle. All things being equal, he would have rather been riding with Maggie, but she wouldn't have been strong enough to pick him up that way.

"What about Boyd?" Dugan shouted over his shoulder.

"Dead!" Longarm replied. "Or he soon will be, the double-crossing son of a bitch!"

The riders had already reached the edge of town. They thundered on out of the settlement, leaving Camden behind them as they fled into the Colorado night.

And at least for the moment, Longarm was still one of them.

Dugan didn't slow his speeding horse until the town was several miles behind them. The fires had been visible for a long way over the prairie, but the outlaws had covered enough distance so that now there wasn't even a glow visible in the sky to the west.

As Dugan brought his mount to a halt, he said over his shoulder to Longarm, "Slide down, Polk. This animal's got to get some rest."

That was true. The horse had been carrying double ever since the getaway from Camden, and both Longarm and Dugan were big men. The mount had responded gallantly to the challenge, but it had to be exhausted.

"You can ride with me, Custis," Maggie offered.

"Much obliged," Longarm said. "We'd better rest all

these horses, though. We're liable to have to make a run for it again, before we get back to the hideout."

Jim Kimmel swung down from his saddle and turned toward Longarm, and as he did so he brought up the gun he'd palmed from his holster. "You're mighty free with that hideout talk, mister," he grated as he eared back the hammer of the Colt. "What the hell happened back there? Why'd you hit me unless you were tryin' to double-cross us too?"

Longarm stared at him incredulously and demanded, "What the devil are you talking about? It was Baxter who walloped you, not me."

"Jim, please," Maggie said. "Put your gun down."

"Take it easy, Jim," Dugan ordered. He looked at Longarm. "But you've got some explaining to do, Polk."

"I don't know why the hell everybody's jumping on me," Longarm said angrily. There was nothing he could do now except run the bluff. "Kimmel and I were riding down one of those alleys when Baxter stepped out behind us and clouted him with a two-by-four. He got me too, the son of a bitch."

Kimmel frowned. The moon had finally come up, and in its silvery illumination, Longarm could see how skeptical the outlaw still looked. "How come he didn't gag you like he did me?" Kimmel asked.

"How in blazes should I know? Maybe he decided he didn't have time. I didn't know anything after he knocked me out of the saddle until I woke up and saw you laying there like you were dead. I got up and went looking for Baxter." Longarm gave a grim laugh. "I found him, and I reckon he wished I hadn't."

"We saw the end of that as we were leaving the bank," Dugan said. "Pretty cold-blooded, gunning a man like that. I'm a mite surprised a writer could do it."

"I want my share of the money," Longarm snapped. "You did get the loot from the bank, didn't you?"

"Some of it," Maggie said. "We had to hurry. Two of

the explosions didn't go off like they were supposed to, and the other two weren't as powerful as they should have been."

"Baxter. He must've stopped them."

Dugan asked, "Why would he do that?"

Longarm turned over another card. "Because he was a railroad detective. Admitted as much to me when he thought he had the drop on me. His real name wasn't Baxter either. It was Boyd, Dan Boyd."

Ed Chester cursed. "I've heard of Boyd. Deke and me had a cousin who rode with Lew Stanton's gang up in the Wind River country. A U.S. marshal name of Boyd busted up that bunch with the help of some local lawmen."

Kimmel slowly lowered his gun and used his other hand to rub his jaw as he frowned in thought. "Yeah, I reckon I've heard about that too," he said after a moment. "The same lawman went after ol' Jake Walsh and some fella named Lorrimer. I recollect the stories. But he was a federal marshal, not a railroad detective."

Longarm shrugged and said, "Boyd told me he'd retired from being a marshal. Guess working for the railroad pays better."

Kimmel holstered his gun. "All right, maybe you're tellin' the truth after all, Polk. But you can't blame me for thinkin' you were the one who hit me. I never saw it coming."

"Neither did I, Jim."

"All right," Dugan said. "The main thing is, Baxter or Boyd or whatever the hell his name was won't be bothering us again. The horses have rested long enough. We'd better get moving again. I don't like the way only two of those explosions went off like they were supposed to. There could be a posse after us already if the townies got the fires under control."

Longarm hoped that wasn't the case. Improbable though it might be, he had come through the chaos back in Camden and was still a member of the gang. The others might still have a few suspicions about him, but the fact that they had seen him shoot down Boyd would go a long way toward making them believe he was one of them.

It was a good thing Boyd had thought of the plan so quickly, and that Longarm had caught on right away.

Of course, they hadn't been able to prevent the gang from robbing the bank, but with Longarm still on the inside, there was always a chance that money could be recovered later for its rightful owners. And he could still act to prevent the raid on the Denver Mint and perhaps even uncover the traitor inside the Mint who was undoubtedly responsible for telling Dugan about the boxcar full of old money. All in all, not the best night's work he had ever done, Longarm thought . . . but it was far from the worst too.

"You take the saddle," Maggie told him as he turned toward her and her horse. "I'll ride behind you."

"You sure about that?" Longarm asked.

She nodded. "I don't mind. I can do that easier than you can."

"All right," he agreed. He took the reins in his hand, grasped the saddlehorn, and swung up onto the animal's back. He reached down, clasped wrists with Maggie, and helped her up. When she was settled behind him, she slipped her arms around his waist.

"There," she said. "Isn't this better?"

He felt the softness of her breasts against his back, and he had to grin. "It's fine. Mighty pleasant, in fact."

"Let's go," Dugan called. He led out, and the others fell in behind him.

Longarm heeled Maggie's horse into a ground-eating trot. He was already looking forward to getting back to the hideout.

It had taken a day and a half, maybe a little more, to reach Camden. Dugan pushed them harder on the way back. The gang rode all night, stopping again only when the sky was gray with the approach of dawn. They rested the horses for an hour this time, then were back in the saddle. Dugan kept up the pace all day. Several times, Maggie rested her head against Longarm's back and dozed off. Once, she drifted into such a sound sleep that she would have fallen off the horse had he not reached back to grab her when he felt her slipping.

Longarm kept an eye on their backtrail, as did all the others. There was no dust rising to signify pursuit, but that didn't prompt Dugan to slow down any. Finally, late in the afternoon, they reached the long cliff and rode along it until they came to the hidden tunnel into the valley. The sun had set by the time they got there, and the interior of the tunnel was stygian. The group had to proceed carefully through it, feeling their way along.

When they emerged from the other end, however, the lighted windows of the cabins were visible, and those yellow glows were welcome sights indeed.

"Simon?" Luke Sims called from the shadows of the trees where he was guarding the tunnel entrance. "Is that you?"

"It's us, all right," Dugan replied. "Deke better have the coffee on."

"Did you take the bank?" Luke called eagerly.

"Damn right we did!" Dugan didn't bother explaining that the haul had been smaller than expected because of the things that had gone wrong. He slapped his saddlebags. "Got your share right here."

The young outlaw let out a whoop. "Go on in," he told them. "I'll fire off a couple of rounds so Deke'll know you're coming."

Luke's Winchester cracked twice as he fired it at the stars. Dugan, Maggie, Longarm, and the others rode on toward the cabins.

Deke Chester greeted them just as effusively. "I thought you might be back tonight," he said as he moved among the group, taking the reins from them so he could lead their

169

horses into the corral. "Got ham and grits and coffee on the stove. Help yourself."

"You're a good man, Deke," Dugan said, clapping him on the back.

The gang went into the cabin, Longarm among them. He'd had a few pieces of jerky and a couple of hard biscuits, all gnawed while he was riding over the past thirty or so hours, and as he smelled the food, he realized how hungry he was.

"Sit down," Maggie said. "I'll bring you something to eat."

"You don't have to wait on me," Longarm told her.

"No, it's all right," she said with a tired smile. "I haven't had anybody to fuss over for a long time, not since . . . Well, just sit down, Custis. Please."

Not since her husband had gone off to prison, where he'd gotten himself killed. That was what she meant, Longarm thought. He did as she asked and seated himself at the table. Maggie filled two plates and brought them over, then went back to the stove for coffee.

She sat down beside him and they dug in, eating hungrily, washing down the food with Deke Chester's strong, bitter coffee. The others were doing the same. There wasn't much conversation in the cabin. Everyone was too hungry to waste time talking when there was food on the table.

Finally, when everyone was finished eating, Dugan and Kimmel got the saddlebags they had brought into the cabin and dropped them on the table amidst the empty plates and cups. "Time we have a look-see at what we got," Dugan announced. He upended the bags and let a pile of string-tied bundles of currency slide out.

There were loud, raucous comments from the outlaws as Dugan counted the loot. When he was done, he announced, "Forty-three thousand, eight hundred seventy-four. That's over forty-three hundred apiece for you boys."

Longarm frowned. "Wait a minute. The divvy ought to be more than that."

"Double shares go to me and Maggie," Dugan said. "That's the way it's always been, Polk. Take it or leave it."

Longarm hesitated a moment, then shrugged. "Don't guess it really matters. I'd have gone along even if I'd known about the split ahead of time."

"I figure we'll pick up at least a quarter of a million when we hit the Mint," Dugan said. He grinned at Longarm. "How long would it take you to earn twenty-five grand writing for *Harper's Weekly*, Polk?"

"Too long," Longarm agreed. "This is better."

"Damn right." Dugan turned to Kimmel. "Jim, bring out that bottle of who-hit-John you've got stashed. It's time we had a drink to celebrate. Even if not everything went the way it was supposed to, we still made a good haul, and we got rid of the viper in our midst, thanks to Polk here."

Kimmel fetched the bottle and splashed whiskey in everybody's coffee cup. Dugan raised his and said, "Here's to the fine art of bank robbing, boyos!"

Along with the others, Longarm echoed the toast and downed the shot of fiery liquor. Then he put the empty cup on the table and said, "It's been a long couple of days. Reckon I'll turn in."

"No need to sleep outside tonight," Dugan told him. "I think you've earned the right to stay wherever you want, Polk." He glanced at Maggie and repeated, "Wherever you want."

Longarm looked at her, and despite the weariness etched on her face, he saw wanting in her eyes. Dugan was giving them free rein to conduct their affair in the open. Longarm didn't see any reason not to take advantage of the opportunity.

She sidled over to him and rested her hand on his arm. "Still tired?" she asked.

"Yeah," Longarm replied honestly, "but I reckon I can stay awake for a while."

Chapter 19

Longarm woke up when Maggie started fondling his cock. This was the same way she had woken him every morning during the past two weeks. Instead of opening his eyes, he lay there on his back in the bunk, sprawled lazily like a big cat, enjoying what she was doing to him.

When she had him fully erect, she shifted around so that her knees were on either side of his head and her face was nestled in his groin. She took the head of his shaft in her mouth and ran her tongue all the way around it.

Longarm opened his eyes then so he could see her lower regions poised right above his face. He slipped his hands up so that he could grip the cheeks of her bottom and gently pull them apart, fully exposing the moist folds of her femaleness just below the valley between her buttocks. He lifted his head so that he could spear her wet center with his tongue.

Maggie's hips thrust against him. She swallowed more of his shaft and started sucking harder. Longarm kept lapping her, using his lips, tongue, and occasionally a nip from his teeth to drive her into more and more of a frenzy. He was rock-hard and ready to shoot off, but he controlled himself with an effort so that Maggie could reach her own culmination. He prodded her along by slipping a finger into the tight brown ring of her bottom.

She cried out around his shaft and took even more of it into her mouth. As her thighs clamped around his head and her juices flooded him, he stopped fighting his own release and allowed it to happen. He filled Maggie's mouth to the brim, emptying himself in one convulsive spasm after another.

Maggie's muscles went limp as she let Longarm's softening shaft slip out of her mouth. Both of them were covered with a fine sheen of sweat. The June days had grown warm, even early in the morning like this.

They were alone in the smaller of the two cabins. The rest of the gang had moved into the larger one, at Dugan's suggestion. Longarm suspected that there had been a little jealousy and resentment on the part of Luke Sims and Bob Hardaway, since they were both young and had had crushes on Maggie themselves. The Chester brothers and Jim Kimmel were a lot more interested in money than they were in any particular woman. They knew that if a gent had enough cash, there were plenty of women in the world who could be had for the taking.

Dugan was a different story. Longarm had tried to figure him out, and the only conclusion he could come to was that Dugan regarded Maggie more as a sister than anything else. Evidently he thought he was honoring the memory of his friendship with Timothy Flynn by not pursuing her himself. At the same time, he wanted Maggie to be happy, and being with Longarm obviously made her happy. She had the sort of glow about her that Longarm had seen all too seldom in the females he had known.

A fella could get to liking this sort of life, Longarm thought sleepily as he lay there with Maggie lying on top of him. He stroked her bottom, then ran his hand over the smooth skin of her back. If she was a cat, she'd have been purring right about now, he told himself. It was so easy to just give himself over to the sensations he was experiencing. . . .

Too damned easy. Too easy to forget that he was a man with a job to do.

And that job was coming soon. According to Dugan, they were all leaving the hideout today to head for Denver.

"We won't be coming back here, so there's no need to leave any guards," Dugan had explained the night before. "We'll be heading west instead, and I don't figure on stopping until we get to San Francisco. Maybe not even then. I hear there are tropical islands out in the Pacific Ocean where a man can live like a king."

"That sounds good to me, Simon," Kimmel had said with a grin. "Can we each have our island?"

Dugan had whooped with laughter and slapped Kimmel on the back. "Damn right, Jimbo!"

Maggie had stayed quiet while the others were engaging in lurid speculation about what they would do with their share of the money. Longarm had wondered at the time what her plans were. Now, as she shifted around on the bunk so that she lay pressed against his long, muscular body, she sighed and said, "A week from now we'll be on a ship bound for New York."

"We will?" Longarm said in surprise.

"That's where I want to go after we get to California. Simon and the others can find themselves an island if they want to, but I plan on us spending the rest of our lives in some big city where we can be comfortable and where no one will ever find us."

"You keep on saying *we* and *us*," Longarm pointed out. "We ain't hashed out what's going to happen after we hit the Mint."

Maggie lifted her head so that she could look at him. A frown creased her forehead. "I assumed we'd be together," she said. "I love you, Custis."

As if that was all it took, Longarm thought.

It didn't matter what plans she made, he reminded him-

174

self. The gang wasn't going to get away with robbing the Mint. Longarm was going to see to that. As tempting as it was to give himself over to the moment and forget about everything that had happened before, there was no denying that Maggie was at least partially responsible for the deaths of more than half a dozen people. And if she set off more explosions in downtown Denver to provide a distraction for the gang's robbery of the mint, the death toll was sure to rise.

So it didn't matter a damn if she loved him and if maybe—just maybe—under different circumstances he could have loved her too. He had a job to do.

"New York it is," he heard himself saying as he rested a hand on her blond hair and pulled her close to him again. "New York . . ."

Longarm used part of his share of the loot from the Camden job to buy himself a dark gray suit and a pearl gray Stetson in one of the smaller towns as the gang rode toward Denver. He imagined he looked considerably different wearing the new duds, though it was hard to disguise his height, his deeply tanned skin, and the distinctive longhorn mustache. He didn't want anybody recognizing him and calling out, "Howdy Marshal!" as the gang rode down Colfax Avenue.

They were all dressed up in new clothes now, and Dugan had rented a buggy with a two-horse team from a livery stable on the outskirts of Denver. He and Maggie were riding in it, to all appearances just a well-to-do young couple out on the town. The other six members of the gang, including Longarm, were pretending not to know each other as they converged on the Mint.

The buggy would serve another purpose. The coins produced in the Mint would be too heavy to carry on horseback, but Dugan had placed a large wooden trunk behind the seat of the buggy and planned to fill it with twenty-dollar gold pieces. The gang wouldn't split up the take until

175

after they had made their escape from Denver. The buggy could be abandoned then.

It wasn't going to come to that, Longarm told himself again. Boyd had surely carried the warning to Billy Vail as Longarm had asked him to, and Vail would make sure that the robbers had a warm welcome waiting for them. Longarm just hoped that waiting the two weeks hadn't caused anybody to let down their guard.

Dugan maneuvered the buggy to the curb and brought it to a stop across the street from the Mint. All along the block, the other members of the gang dismounted. Maggie and Dugan got out of the buggy, Dugan taking her arm like the proud husband he was pretending to be. Maggie smiled brightly at him, looking beautiful in her new clothes. They started to stroll along the street.

They passed Longarm where he was lounging against a lamppost. Dugan paused to light his pipe and used that to cover his low-voiced comment to Longarm. "Don't forget the rendezvous," he said.

"Not likely," Longarm grunted.

"We'll all be there for the split, even Skillman."

"Who's that?"

"Fella who works at the Mint. He's the one who passed me all the information we needed."

Longarm gave a minuscule nod, being careful not to let Dugan see his true reaction. He had just about given up on getting Dugan to reveal the inside man's identity. He had been trying subtly for two weeks to pry the name out of the bandit chief. Now, at almost the last moment, Dugan's own garrulous nature finally had given away that vital bit of information.

"Remember, Custis," Maggie whispered, her lips barely moving. "Remember our plans. . . ."

Then she and Dugan were gone, the two of them strolling into the first building. They would find an out-of-the-way corner, and she would plant the first of her dynamite and nitroglycerine bombs. Before she was finished, the deadly

176

bundles would be stashed in buildings all up and down the street. When they went off, it would be like an artillery barrage striking downtown Denver, and the last thing anybody would be worried about was somebody being bold enough to rob the Mint.

A man in a light gray suit and a cream-colored Stetson went into the building behind Maggie and Dugan, walking quickly with his head down as if intent on his business. He paused, though, as he went past Longarm, and a swift glance up caused his eyes to meet Longarm's. Then he was gone, so fast that Longarm had barely had time to recognize Dan Boyd.

The trap was being sprung, Longarm realized. Vail probably had deputy marshals and special agents spread all up and down the street, ready to grab the would-be robbers. They would be waiting now for the sign from Longarm to move in—that is, if Boyd had set everything up with Vail as he and Longarm had talked about while they were fighting in the street in Camden.

Boyd was probably planning to trail along after Maggie and Dugan and defuse all those sticks of dynamite. If he was careful—and by this time, Longarm expected nothing less from Boyd—they wouldn't notice him following them. Longarm decided to play things out just a little while longer. Maggie had another vial of nitroglycerine on the cord around her neck, and Longarm hadn't had a chance to switch the stuff this time. He wanted her to use all of it setting up the blasts before any trouble started. He wasn't going to take a chance that the vial might blow up while Maggie was still wearing it when things got a little rough.

That was his plan anyway, and it might have worked—with a little bit of luck that Longarm didn't get.

He was still leaning against the lamppost when Maggie and Dugan came out of the building. Their eyes flickered toward him for a second, and he read the message there: The dynamite and the nitroglycerine had been successfully hidden. Even now, a long fuse was sputtering away . . . unless Boyd had already gotten to it and stopped it. Dugan and Maggie turned to walk on down the street.

That was when a hand came down on Longarm's left shoulder and a high-pitched voice said loudly, "Marshal Long! I almost didn't recognize you. When did you get back into town? Remember me? E. E. Polk?"

Longarm stiffened in horror as the little journalist yapped at him. A few feet away, both Maggie and Dugan had stopped short, and Dugan was looking back over his shoulder. His eyes met Longarm's again as Polk added, "Where's your badge? I thought you always wore it when you were here in town."

"Oh, shit!" Longarm exclaimed as his left arm swept out and slammed into Polk's chest. Polk went flying backward, his arms windmilling wildly. At the same time, Longarm's right hand flashed across his body to the Colt in the cross-draw rig. That was as much of a signal as the deputies waiting along the street were going to get.

For a thin-shaved heartbeat of time as he grasped the butt of his gun, Longarm hoped he was right about Boyd setting up an ambush with Billy Vail. If he didn't have anybody backing his play . . .

Too late to worry about that now. In a smooth blur of motion, he drew his gun and brought it up.

But Dugan was fast too, one hand darting under his coat while the other grabbed Maggie's arm and jerked her in front of him to use as a shield. Longarm cursed as he saw what Dugan was doing. Down the street, a couple of shots blasted, and somebody yelled. Instantly, the broad downtown avenue was a battleground as deputies opened fire on the outlaws. Boyd must have given the authorities descriptions of every member of the gang.

Maggie cried out in pain as Dugan jerked on her arm. Longarm managed to keep his finger from pressing the trigger of the Colt. He couldn't fire with Maggie between him and Dugan. Dugan didn't have to worry about that. The pistol in his hand cracked wickedly, sending a slug sizzling past Longarm's ear.

Maggie drove her elbow back into Dugan's belly, taking him by surprise. That loosened his grip on her arm enough for her to twist around and claw at his face. She was still in the way of a shot, though, so Longarm couldn't fire as Dugan backhanded her viciously. Then his hand dropped to the bosom of her dress and ripped it open. His fingers closed around the vial of nitroglycerine and jerked it free, snapping the thong around her neck. Maggie cried out in fear.

Dugan flung the vial toward Longarm.

Longarm's eyes widened as he saw the vial coming at him. He had little or no chance to catch it before it smashed onto the sidewalk at his feet, and that impact would set off a blast that wouldn't leave enough of him to scrape up.

Dan Boyd came out of nowhere, flying across the sidewalk in a diving lunge that brought his outstretched hand underneath the vial. He caught it, juggling the smooth glass container for an instant before it settled securely into his palm. He sprawled on the sidewalk, but was able to keep his arm raised, the nitroglycerine cradled gently in his grip.

"Get Dugan!" he yelled at Longarm.

"Maggie! Get down!" Longarm shouted.

Too late. Dugan was already squeezing the trigger again. As his gun blasted, the bullet ripped across Maggie's side. She staggered and fell. Longarm felt something twinge inside him at the sight of the blood on her dress. He triggered the Colt, felt the familiar buck of the weapon against his palm. The slug drove into Dugan's left shoulder, spinning him halfway around but failing to knock him off his feet. His face contorting with pain and rage, Dugan fired again, the sound of the shot blending with Longarm's second one. Dugan's bullet ricocheted off the sidewalk, while Longarm's drove cleanly into the outlaw leader's chest. Dugan staggered, his eyes widening with the realization of what had just happened. His arm sagged, and though he tried to bring the gun up for one last shot, his strength was running out of him too fast.

Dugan fell, pitching face-forward on the sidewalk.

Longarm was pretty sure Dugan was dead, but he had to make certain. He stepped quickly past Maggie, and his foot lashed out to kick away the gun Dugan had just dropped. Longarm knelt to check Dugan for a pulse.

"Miz Flynn! Hold it!"

That was Boyd's voice, and the alarm in it made Longarm jerk his head around. Maggie had managed to get back onto her feet, and she was half-staggering, half-running toward the mouth of a nearby alley.

"Maggie! Come back here!" Longarm yelled.

As he surged to his feet and ran after her, he was aware that the shooting elsewhere on the street had stopped. He hoped that meant the other members of the gang had been either killed or captured. Right now, however, his main concern was Maggie. She needed a sawbones for that bullet wound.

She was halfway down the alley by the time he reached it. "Maggie!" he called again. "Wait!"

She stumbled to a halt and turned to face him. Her left arm was clamped to her side where the bullet had creased her. Longarm could tell from the stain on her dress that the wound was bleeding freely, but with prompt medical attention, it shouldn't be too serious. But she had to come with him now.

As he walked along the alley toward her, the Colt held down at his side, she said shakily, "You lied to me!"

"I'm sorry, Maggie," he said, and meant it. "I wish there had been some other way."

"You bastard! I loved you!"

"I know," Longarm said.

Maggie's right hand went into the ripped bosom of her dress and came out clutching something that Longarm couldn't make out in the dim light of the alley. "I brought some extra soup this time," she said as she raised her arm.

"I was worried about it not being powerful enough after what happened in Camden."

Because he had substituted water for the real thing, Longarm realized. He was about to tell her that when she said, "I won't go to prison like Tim."

Longarm had been afraid at first she intended to throw the stuff at him, but now he realized too late that she had something else in mind. Her fingers opened, and he saw the glass vial dropping from them and falling toward the flagstones of the alley. He was still too far away from her. He knew he couldn't get there in time to catch the vial, and this time there was no one else to make a last-second catch. He opened his mouth to shout, "Maggie! Noooooo . . . !"

Then he heard the faint tinkle of breaking glass, and it was the last thing he heard for a long time.

Chapter 20

"Every time I see you," E. E. Polk said, "guns start to go off and you wind up knocking me down. Now I find out that you even appropriated my name without permission in order to infiltrate a group of desperadoes!"

"Yeah," Longarm said, "but it'll make a pretty good story for you, won't it?" He threw back what was left of the Maryland rye in his glass.

"Well, yes, I suppose so, but still . . ."

"Take my advice, Mr. Polk," Dan Boyd said. "Just be glad it was Longarm and not you there in the midst of those outlaws."

"That's right," Billy Vail added. "I reckon sometimes it's better to just write about things than it is to live through them yourself."

The four men were sitting at a table in the back corner of a Denver saloon. Longarm's left arm was in a black cloth sling, his face was marked with the same sort of fading bruises that had made the rest of his body a veritable rainbow, and he still had a little trouble hearing out of his left ear sometimes. But he was confident that he would be back to normal in no time. After all, only a week had passed since he'd almost been caught in that explosion.

He'd been in the hospital for three days, then had holed

up with a bottle of Tom Moore for four more in his rented room on the other side of Cherry Creek. Tonight was the first time he had ventured out, and he had done so only at the insistence of Dan Boyd, who had been a regular visitor.

A regular annoyance, that was what Boyd was, Longarm had thought several times. He didn't need any reminders of everything that had happened. It was all too clear in his mind as it was.

And what the hell had possessed Boyd and Vail to invite E. E. Polk along tonight?

"I'm leaving Denver tomorrow, you know," Polk said now, as if he had heard the question that was going through Longarm's mind. "I certainly appreciate this send-off, gentlemen."

"You write some good stories, hear?" Vail told him.

"Just leave me out of them," Boyd said. "I might need to resurrect that mysterious gunman known as Baxter sometime in the future."

"You ought to start carrying a marshal's badge again, that's what you ought to do," Vail said. "I'd hire you to work out of my office in a minute, Dan."

Boyd laughed. "Not hardly, Billy. I've done all the star packing I'm of a mind to do."

"It's a damn waste of talent, that's what it is," Vail said, shaking his head regretfully.

Longarm poured another drink.

"You know, it's a shame about Mrs. Flynn," Polk said. "From everything the two of you have told me, she wasn't as bad as Dugan and the others."

"She was a bank robber," Longarm said flatly. He drank half the rye.

"Yes, but she wasn't motivated by greed."

"Doesn't matter."

"You know," Vail said, "there was a door off that alley right beside the crater that got blown in it. And we never found any sign of the woman except for some blood."

"She was already bleeding from the gunshot wound," Boyd pointed out.

"Yeah," Vail mused. "That's what I was thinking."

Longarm finished the drink and stood up. He was still stone-cold sober, but he said, "That's enough for me."

"Are you sure?" Vail asked.

"I'm certain."

Boyd started to get to his feet. "I'll walk you back to your boardinghouse—"

"The hell you will," Longarm snapped. His tone eased a little as he went on. "I'll be fine. You and Billy stay here and give ol' E. E. the send-off he's got coming."

"Custis . . ." Vail began.

Longarm picked up his hat from the table, clapped it on his head, and turned toward the door, giving his companions a wave of farewell as he did so. He hoped they would stay where they were, and was grateful when they did.

He made his way out of the smoky interior of the saloon and stepped out into a warm, cloudy summer night. Even here in the city, even a little heavy with moisture, the air smelled good on a night like this. Longarm took a deep breath of it and then turned toward Cherry Creek.

He had taken only a few steps when he stopped short. The gas lamps along the street were all lit, and a couple of blocks away, a woman was walking toward him. Longarm couldn't make out her face at this distance, but the lamplight suddenly shone on blond hair underneath her hat. Longarm felt his heart slugging hard in his chest.

Then she turned a corner and was gone from his sight.

For a moment, he thought about breaking into a run and chasing her down. But she couldn't be who she had looked like for a moment. It was just such a long chance. . . .

Longarm drew a deep breath and said aloud, "Go home, old son. Go home."

There were some ghosts that a man just shouldn't ought to chase, and anyway, it was starting to rain.

184

Watch for

LONGARM AND THE NEVADA BELLY DANCER

257th novel in the exciting LONGARM series
from Jove

Coming in April!

**Explore the exciting Old West with one
of the men who made it wild!**

JAKE LOGAN
TODAY'S HOTTEST ACTION WESTERN!

☐ SLOCUM AND THE LAST GASP #234	0-515-12355-2/$4.99
☐ SLOCUM AND THE MINER'S JUSTICE #235	0-515-12371-4/$4.99
☐ SLOCUM AT HELL'S ACRE #236	0-515-12391-9/$4.99
☐ SLOCUM AND THE WOLF HUNT #237	0-515-12413-3/$4.99
☐ SLOCUM AND THE BARONESS #238	0-515-12436-2/$4.99
☐ SLOCUM AND THE COMANCHE PRINCESS #239	0-515-12449-4/$4.99
☐ SLOCUM AND THE LIVE OAK BOYS #240	0-515-12467-2/$4.99
☐ SLOCUM#241: SLOCUM AND THE BIG THREE	0-515-12484-2/$4.99
☐ SLOCUM #242: SLOCUM AT SCORPION BEND	0-515-12510-5/$4.99
☐ SLOCUM AND THE BUFFALO HUNTER #243	0-515-12518-0/$4.99
☐ SLOCUM AND THE YELLOW ROSE OF TEXAS #244	0-515-12532-6/$4.99
☐ SLOCUM AND THE LADY FROM ABILINE #245	0-515-12555-5/$4.99
☐ SLOCUM GIANT: SLOCUM AND THE THREE WIVES	0-515-12569-5/$5.99
☐ SLOCUM AND THE CATTLE KING #246	0-515-12571-7/$4.99
☐ SLOCUM #247: DEAD MAN'S SPURS	0-515-12613-6/$4.99
☐ SLOCUM #248: SHOWDOWN AT SHILOH	0-515-12659-4/$4.99
☐ SLOCUM AND THE KETCHEM GANG #249	0-515-12686-1/$4.99
☐ SLOCUM AND THE JERSEY LILY #250	0-515-12706-X/$4.99
☐ SLOCUM AND THE GAMBLER'S WOMAN #251	0-515-12733-7/$4.99
☐ SLOCUM AND THE GUNRUNNERS #252	0-515-12754-X/$4.99
☐ SLOCUM AND THE NEBRASKA STORM #253	0-515-12769-8/$4.99
☐ SLOCUM'S CLOSE CALL #254 (4/00)	0-515-12789-2/$4.99

Prices slightly higher in Canada

Payable in U.S. funds only. No cash/COD accepted. Postage & handling: U.S./CAN $2.75 for one book, $1.00 for each additional, not to exceed $6.75; Int'l $5.00 for one book, $1.00 each additional. We accept Visa, Amex, MC ($10.00 min.), checks ($15.00 fee for returned checks) and money orders. Call 800-788-6262 or 201-933-9292, fax 201-896-8569; refer to ad # 202 (12/99)

Penguin Putnam Inc.
P.O. Box 12289, Dept. B
Newark, NJ 07101-5289
Please allow 4-6 weeks for delivery
Foreign and Canadian delivery 6-8 weeks

Bill my: ☐ Visa ☐ MasterCard ☐ Amex _____ (expires)

Card# _____

Signature _____

Bill to:

Name _____

Address _____ City _____

State/ZIP _____ Daytime Phone # _____

Ship to:

Name _____ Book Total $ _____

Address _____ Applicable Sales Tax $ _____

City _____ Postage & Handling $ _____

State/ZIP _____ Total Amount Due $ _____

This offer subject to change without notice.